BOOK TWO

Which is a dirge for the woman who was Eleonore and so, we find her...

1.

ELEONORE SMITH WITH HER SMALL CHUBBY HANDS and pink toned skin and that no-color hair—for it was no color which could be named, not blonde, nor red, nor black, nor brown, nor any other color—sat in the front seat of the old Chevy truck which her husband drove and looked over at him, the dashboard light illuminating the furled curves of his face. His mouth was tight and small. He clutched the steering wheel and breathed through his nose.

The man hadn't spoken but a few words since they'd left his brother's house in Salt Lake City earlier that afternoon. And now, she pulled a pastry wrapped in tissue from her pocket and pushed it into her mouth as she went over in her head the events of the day—and the events of their lives together—up to that moment.

She was lucky to have had him. She knew that. In school, all those years ago, she couldn't talk to anyone, and even up into the seventh grade, she'd wet her pants in class more than once—too shy to ask the teacher for the bathroom pass. Boys grimaced at her or laughed to each other when she was called on by the teacher or when she tried to ask them for a pencil. It was not for a lack of looks.

She was pretty—Eleonore had good skin and light feminine features. And she was strong from her life on her elderly parents' farm and short. Boys thought of her in ways, but not the way she or any girl would have wanted them to. The country girl stuttered terribly. And she was skittish, leaning her head back and looking down her nose with her giant eyes like a scared little rabbit.

She daydreamed. She wished for something more.

And perhaps, more than the awkward adolescence she endured, it was her place and the life she had in relation to her family that formed her. That is what primed her to feel that Beau was a blessing. For when the stout young girl walked home from school every afternoon, Eleonore's waning parents left her with the chores of tending to the animals and chopping firewood and all the rest which had to be done.

She sat on her stool and milked the cow. She fed the chickens. And the imaginations she entertained during those hours alone in the barn or in the field were imaginations that filled her being with anticipation and a heel-bouncing giddiness. They were thoughts of love and marriage, of being someone's wife. She wanted love like any girl does. She wanted marriage.

Her brothers and sisters were all adults and gone from the house by then.[1] A number of them had children as old as she was. It had been a surprise when her mother—who had become morbidly obese in the last half of her life—went to the hospital complaining of pain in her stomach,[2] only to produce the infant Eleonore. Everyone was surprised. It had been 14 years since the eleventh—and what was supposed to be the very last—child was born. Eleonore was the twelfth.

---

[1] Only one of Eleonore's siblings was less than two decades older than she was.
[2] Eleonore's mother and father assumed the pain was a kidney stone or appendicitis.

They raised her in the church, the Mormon church. She could recite long passages from the King James bible and the Pearl of Great Price and the Doctrine and Covenants, but her favorite was the Book of Mormon itself, which she hugged against her chest everywhere she went. It was a thing known to Eleonore—even at a very young age—that the farm and all its acres would be sold upon the death of her parents and all but a stipend for the children would be given to the church. Eleonore wouldn't have it any other way.

Her life was devoted to God, yet she could not help but feel that her life was passing her by in that place called Nephi, Utah. Things were missing from her. She wanted love. She wanted to be loved, but she didn't have a single friend. There'd never been—and would never be—a sleepover for her in her life. Even laughter seemed absent from her existence. Her folks seldom smiled, old as they were.

So, when Beau Smith—the black haired and harelipped twin brother of the valedictorian Blaine Smith—stood next to her locker in February of senior year, clumsily stuck in a stutter himself, and finally blurted out the question,

"Will you be my valentine?" she turned red and smiled and nodded wildly. There was no other thing for her to answer, and there was no other way for Eleonore's life to go. This was it. This was the will of her God.

AND THEY COURTED. He bought her ice cream after school. It wasn't uncommon for him to be waiting for her in the parking lot before school, and when summer came, he picked her up from her new job at the library after work on his bike. Eleonore talked with him and laughed. She could, then. Her stutter was going away, and out of high school, Beau Smith had begun to grow a thick black mustache to hide his harelip.

Beau seemed perfect, no in any actual sense. No. Beau was flawed in many obvious ways with his poor posture and shyness and irritability. But he was perfect in a certain sense. Hardly a man, he fit her ideas of what God had for her and what was right. He was Mormon like she was. He had a big family like she did. So much seemed right.

And there was never a moment of doubt or uneasiness in Eleonore about him, except when his hands touched hers. They were big and strong. The fingernails were clean, and everything looked okay, but when his palms grabbed the skin on the back of her wrists or rubbed her neck, they were warm and soft and weak. Worst of all, they were perpetually moist. Something about them made her shake her head and shudder. Even a thought of those warm feeble blobs at the ends of his arms put knots in her stomach. But she smiled when he grabbed her elbows and looked at her.

Now, the leaves were changing. And Beau returned home from Fort Sill in Oklahoma in his service uniform, a military cap on his head. They went for ice cream at their favorite place. Beau knelt at her feet. And his giant hands shook with the box and held the ring out to her. She squealed and covered her mouth and said yes. There was no other thing for her to answer, and there was no other way for Eleonore's life to go.

Their ceremony was small. Eleonore's father slept in his wheelchair through the wedding. Her mother couldn't make it out of the hospital, at all. It was that night, after the tiny and quiet wedding reception at Beau's aunt's house, that Eleonore's happiness about her new husband

and the children they would have and all that their beautiful future held disappeared. They would disappear. And those things would never come back. She learned that night what heartbreak was, what it was like being crushed and suffocated in silence, and in the 17 years of their quiet and childless marriage, they'd never mentioned it, not even once.

THIS MORNING, though, they'd woken up and left their home in Idaho for Nephi before the sun rose to visit Beau's brother and his family. It was a yearly event for them. They celebrated their mid-December birthdays together like the twins they were, only Beau's brother Blaine and his family had flourished.

They had seven kids. All of them were athletic and top of their classes and beautiful, and the oldest one would start college the following year. It was the only time Eleonore got away from their little farmhouse—sitting on 87 acres of rugged rock and thistle and pine trees which they'd purchased outright almost two decades before—in the mountains 100 miles west of Pocatello, and it was the one of the few human interactions she had experienced since she and Beau had moved out there.

Now, as she sat there in the front seat of the truck, studying the dark and grumbling figure in the cab across from her and brushed crumbs of the pastry she'd just eaten from her lap, Eleonore nodded and understood why he was upset. She remembered, now. It was the moment their small niece had laughingly asked Beau,

"Why don't you have any children, Uncle Beau? Huh? Don't you want children?" His shoulders had slumped that very instant. His face had changed. It hurt her, too, but she'd grown accustomed to the shame of being childless. It was less humiliating than the touchless marriage bed they shared, and Beau grunted to her,

"I'm pulling over here."

"For what, Beau?"

"For to relieve myself...is that okay?"

"Oh. Of course, it is."

ELEONORE STOOD IN THE SMALL AND FLICKERING lamppost light that buzzed high above her. The night bit her skin, a black cold. There was, in the grass and snow where Beau had pulled over and the truck ran, a lonely and quiet washhouse.

It had once been a pump house, decades before that night, for an old farm. And the walls sagged and leaned and were made out of shoddy brown brick painted white. And it had existed just like that and in the same place—some 35 minutes from the gate onto their easement road—for all of the years that they'd been in the quiet country. The small building had a hole in a square of tiled floor for travelers to squat over and a small, dirty sink. Beau walked off toward a tree sticking up out of the snow and stood with his back to her as he sighed. He leaned back. His head relaxed. Steam rose from his collar and head.

Eleonore rubbed her palms on her hips and gripped the fold of fat around her waist with her quickly numbing fingers. She was moving toward the washhouse for herself. And now, she was pausing, caught up and deep in thought. Images of the ugly looks Beau had given her over the years played out in her head, things he'd done or said to thwart her romantic advances. She winced as she remembered him saying that she smelled bad. He said she was fat, once, and that she could have cooked a better dinner. He ignored her.

And at the end of her imaginations—standing

there outside of the truck with her jaw slack—dread filled her chest at the ultimate and worst of those memories, remembering back on herself and Beau—they'd been so young—and how happy she was to have waited her whole life as a virgin to give herself to her husband.

The beauty of that gift—her own untouched body—had always been in giving it. But to have him push her hands away with his own—so warm and wet—left her searching in the dark for his lips with hers. Her new husband turned over and away from her. She whimpered. Eleonore desperately reached out to her spouse, again, in the dark and touched his back. Beau shook her off and breathed out loudly through his nose.

For some hours, she stared up into the room. Her mouth hung open, and she chewed on her finger and sniffed at the tears in her nose and on lips. It was their wedding night.

SHE HADN'T TAKEN MANY STEPS over the dirt pull-off on the side of the road to the bathroom. She was lost in her thoughts. It was getting colder.

The fat woman was stuck, wondering if her husband liked women at all or if he was simply impotent or, perhaps, bore in his mind and body some other unspeakable scar—some internal and otherwise invisible mutilation—that prevented him, though his young wife was willing, and now, Beau was back to the truck and opening the door and calling out to her,

"Eleonore! What is it? Let's go."

"Okay," she breathed out and pinched her long skirt in both hands and took bigger, quicker steps toward the washhouse, moving in an exaggerated waddle, the way she moved with her excess weight.

In her path lay an animal carcass or a discarded pelt. It was white and still, but as Eleonore stood over it, she reached down. She prodded it and now could see the stitching in the seams of a gauzy hairnet and long, shining synthetic fibers of fake blond hair. The thing was a wig.

When she picked it up, hard bits of something cold and wet touched the inside of her fingers and hand, a frozen and murky liquid. And Eleonore moved closer to the door of the small washhouse and pushed it open and grabbed a ball of her skirt's fabric in the other, tossing the wig into the sink and flipping the light switch.

INSIDE OF THE WASHHOUSE, the filament in the bare bulb above her head clicks and glows orange and is putting out light into the small dilapidated space that smells of old urine. It is freezing—perhaps the coldest night Eleonore has seen in some years, somewhere far below zero—and her breath is visible.

Now, Eleonore spooks at the sound of breathing and the smell of something strange—something out of place—perfumy and metallic, and now, as the light comes on, she beholds a body in a thick brown leather coat. Tight white denim covers the legs, one of which is horrifyingly folded behind the body's back. There is a pair of bright red high tops on the feet, and now, Eleonore turns the mangled figure over, slowly. It looks like a boy.

The face is thin and small like a boy's or maybe a woman's and wears a shaggy haircut like a man might have. Eyes are unresponsive. One is open partially, showing only the milky white eyeball. There is a gash in the skin over the other eyebrow, and this person—the broken body Eleonore thinks, now, might be a girl—stinks like rancid liquor and blood and bad breath.

The bottom lip of the victim bleeds or has bled, having been badly split. And Elenore mumbles to the person. She strokes the leather shoulder of the jacket, the way a little girl might pet the thick coat of a deceased wolf or coyote and asks questions. She grabs a thin, lifeless hand.

And now, Eleonore is stiff and sits down on the dirt floor of the washhouse and strokes the hair of this mangled creature and pulls the victim into her lap and is overcome by the sensation that she knows this person, as if this is all something she dreamt in a dream long ago, perhaps as a little girl. And she is horrified to think that somehow the suffering of this wounded—and perhaps dead—thing before her is the making of her own mind, a creature harbored somewhere in her dreams and, now, vomited out into reality to lay bloody and bruised on the ground of that dirty roadside washhouse. It is quiet. She is smeared with blood and the stink. The world outside of the washhouse seems to disappear. There is nothing to Eleonore, now, but her and the lifeless form in her lap.

And for a moment, Eleonore's face turns red. She is almost crying, when a few small moans and the slight gurgling of phlegm escape the girl's—or maybe boy's—mouth. And now, Eleonore stands up and calls out to Beau in the running truck. She waves wildly with her whole arm, and when he gets out, she says,

"Come on! I need your help."

"Help? With what?" He is irritated. He shakes his head.

"There's somebody in here! Somebody hurt!" Her breath has quickly frozen in the white, peach fuzz hairs around her lips. She looks back at the body and studies the rings of black hair. It is clotted with chunks of frozen blood.

"What?" he asks.

"There's a girl in here."

"What girl?" he is stepping around the corner to see. "What are you talking about, Eleonore?"

"It's a boy or a man or…"

Beau stares and looks behind his wife. He stretches his neck to see into the washroom.

"This!" Eleonore shouts, now, and puts her hand over her mouth and points a short finger at a thin and bloody figure with wild black hair, wearing the thick leather jacket, limbs sprawled out on the dirt floor. Eleonore says softly now, "Her… or him… the poor thing."

ELEONORE'S FATHER PASSED onto death peacefully in a third-floor hospital bed while Beau was out of town working for the company with which he took a job after the army. He was in Puerto Rico. They were building some kind of plant on the coast of the island. Sometimes, he was gone for more than a half a year at a time. And she was lonely when Beau was gone. She thought to herself that she was just as lonely when he was around, and now, it was quiet in the room.

Eleonore watched the slowing breaths and her father's grey, creased lips for hours, sitting with her fingers locked over her lap. It took her some time. But soon, she stood at his bed and observed the old man's deceased body. Whatever he had been, he was no longer. She bent over. His forehead wasn't cold or cool or warm when she kissed the papery skin over the bone in his skull.

The girl—not yet 20—wrapped her fingers around the railing of his bed, and the thin band of sliver on the ring finger of her left hand clicked against the metal. It was serene and strange. She whispered over him her thanks for his being a good father, even if he had been a stranger to her, and then she said his name which she had never said in her life and which was Festus. And that was it.[1]

The days following moved slowly. Her brothers and sisters visited her at the small house north of Nephi and told of all the things they'd done in their lives. And some of their children came with their children, one toddler who ran between their legs and screamed and hit his head on the corner of a cabinet and bled and cried and two baldheaded babies who slobbered and looked out from their young mothers' arms.

Only seven of her siblings had shown for the wake and burial of their father. Three were dead. Another—a brother—was stationed in in a base

somewhere outside of Vietnam.

Her oldest brother, though, was there. He stood scared and scary and silent in the corners of her living room with his one hand held up at his side like a deformed talon. And his eyes were sunk and dark. There was talk between Lottie and Dottie, the eldest two of the girls in the family. They said he was on drugs out in northern California and,

"Sleeping in a van on some kind of compound with a bunch hippies. Shame. I've seen some of that on the TV, women all naked and harrier than animals, men with hair longer than the women." The sister named Lottie said and pushed the hair from her eye, sneering and shaking her head.

And on the table, there was a key lime pie which Eleonore had made and from which cut a piece and took to her oldest brother—who held it and looked down at it and

---

[1] Eleonore's mother had deceased the year before.

never ate any of it. No one else did, either, except Eleonore, and before the evening was finished, there were only crumbs of crust in the pan. She sipped cold sweet tea from a glass that was in her hand after that, and the lot of them spoke to each other. They ignored Eleonore and the eldest brother as though they were strangers. And soon, they stood. They were all shuffling and mumbling and said goodbye, before they left the house.

The executor of the deceased couple's estate met them in the morning at his office and stood behind his desk, smiling. There was a contract from some branch of the military which their parents had refused to sign. It was for rights to tap what was suspected to be one of the largest deposits of uranium on the continent. Several million dollars could be theirs to split, if the seven children present signed it. Their military brother had

already agreed over the phone. With nothing more than a shared look, Lottie reached for a pen and the other five stood in line, and only Eleonore hesitated. She was the only one to offer even a moment of thought to it.

She wondered why the property was not going to the church. It was what she always knew would happen. But as she looked around the room and saw the faces of her sisters, Eleonore would not ask. And now, she was signing the paper, too. Beau was back by August that year. He was gone, again. And she found a piece of land up in Idaho for sale by an older and childless couple.

The land came with a few cows. There was a chicken coup and two small barns, one decrepit and empty, the other newly constructed and painted red. By a duck pond in the shade of a hill sat the square redbrick house surrounded by an old garden, shaded by thatches of oak and spruce, and without so much as a word from Beau, Eleonore purchased the property outright. The thing which sold her on the property—aside from its seclusion and size—was a pair of Chinkapin oaks that stood like pillars out of the world—and into Eleonore's—for anyone coming to visit.

THE EASEMENT ROAD WAS LONGER THAN MOST. It could take a whole hour to travel it during the rains of early fall and spring or winter when the snow melted, to get to the house from the red metal gate that faced the small road they were turning off of, now. The mangled woman hung forward in her seat. Eleonore felt more certain as time passed that it was a woman and pinned her back with her elbow from the passenger seat. Beau struggled to shift. It was cramped inside of the truck's cab. The bumps of the rising and dropping road—which had been sitting in disrepair for

some years now—jostled the nameless being between them, and now, Beau whined,

"What's that smell?"

Eleonore shook her head for a moment,

"I don't smell anything," she said and, then, wincingly shook her head, again, and rolled down her window.

It was at the end of the road where their property began and past the Chinkapin oaks that Beau flung open his door and stood splattering vomit on his shoes and pants. He couldn't help Eleonore get the body inside of the house, but the injured stranger was a scant girl. The stocky woman carried the battered girl into the house and on into the bathroom.

Eleonore shut the door. She washed the feces and dried blood from woman's body and hair and face. It was indeed a woman. Eleonore knew that, now, without any doubt. The body was a pathetic sight to see, limp and flopping in her hands. Worse yet was the smushed face barely breathing and only the whites of her under eyes showing.

The purple-splotched and swelling tissue in the woman's face distorted her features. She was monstrous. A dreaded lock of hair—with bits of stone or bone or small animals' teeth integrated into it—hid beneath the medium length hair and slipped through Eleonore's fingers. Lumps from whatever violence she had suffered were forming, a very large one on her head. On her left hand, a great gash of dangling flesh started in her palm. The web of skin between her pinky and ring finger was torn, as if a nail had pierced her and been ripped through the tissue.

And now, Eleonore found herself staring. She couldn't turn away from the shocking appearance of that body—aside from the ways it had been brutalized, she gawked at the hybrid features of a boyishness on the clearly female frame. It was the coarse black hairs on her shins. It was the victim's thighs—the pair of thin but masculine legs with muscle and definition and one badly swollen ankle which had already begun to turn colors.

Wiry patches of hair thick as a child's head stuck out from the girl's armpits. And there were tattoos of birds all over her torso and legs and arms and chest. The big toe and another on the same foot had nails which were opaque and thick and yellowed as if afflicted by some sort of fungal growth. Eleonore had never seen anything like it, certainly not on a woman.

And Eleonore stood. She pressed her lips together and breathed and left for a moment and returned with a nightgown for her charge and dressed her and ran another tub of water to soak the filth from the woman's garments and washed her hands and pulled the woman's arm over the back of her neck and carried her to a bed in the side room. It was in laying the lankier woman down that a breath of air escaped.

Eleonore shook her head at the smell. It was the same stink she'd smelled on the breath of a man named Jerry Hoskins who stood behind her and her parents at church when she was very young, and his singing, while rich and deep and beautiful, broadcast the smell of something rotting deep within him. Her father had it, too, later in his life but not as bad. She knew the condition to be called halitosis and whispered that word to herself and to the deaf-mute sleeper in her arms.

Eleonore left the room. She came back and sat next to the unconscious body studying the wounds, mostly the split of her lip and lump on her head which looked to be painful but not deadly. The cuts on the eye were in a worse spot, but they, also, seemed to be little more than superficial.

So, Eleonore opened a jar of perfumed balm which she had prepared the way her mother had before her and stuck her fingers inside of the container and pushed the salve into the wounds around the girl's eye and over her eyelids. She wiped less of the thick Vaseline-like ointment onto the cut lip, and again, the simple farm woman in her display of compassion pulled another glob of the balm and spread it over the gash in the woman's hand and bound it in the thin, brown gauze of a stocking. Eleonore was soft and slow. It was all done with tremendous care.

And after all of this, Eleonore stood to tuck her wounded patient into bed. But before she did, she studied an amulet hanging from the woman's neck. There was a polished-looking orb of hardened amber which contained a thin, bird bone skull and fastened to it with a beautifully wrapped coil of silver wire was a rugged looking arrowhead made out of nephrite jade and upon that arrowhead was engraved an ancient face and encircled about the face were various arcane characters. It all hung from a loop of leather around her neck.

So, Eleonore pinched the thing in her squatty hand. She lifted it from the clavicle upon which the thing rested and studied it in her fingers. There was a pair of keys—one small and the other of a normal size—strung from the leather, as well, and, again, Eleonore smelled the stink of the girl's breath. She felt the warmth of that body on her own and sighed and tucked the beaten woman into bed. It was more contact than she'd had with anyone in decades. At the door, she stood for a moment and looked back. She clucked her tongue in

pit. Eleonore wiped her forehead.

IN THE LIVING ROOM, Beau held the mantelpiece above the fire place. His posture was that of someone studying a fire, and when his wife came out of the room, he looked at her with a swivel of his head. He looked back at the fire. Now, he felt the shrunken scar tissue in his lip between the bristles of his mustache with a finger and said,

"Well..."

"Well, what?" Eleonore asked.

"Everything okay?"

"I think so," the woman wiped her hands on her dress and moved around the kitchen.

"And what are we doing with her or him or whatever it is, Eleonore?"

"A woman."

"A woman?"

"To be sure..."

"Really?"

Eleonore nodded.

Beau waited and stared and furrowed his brow. He said,

"Well, still... the question remains. What are we doing with her, Eleonore?"

"And don't you know, Beau Smith?"

"I do not!"

"Have you not read the parable of the Good Samaritan? Do you not know it?"

"I have. And I do. Is that what this is?"

"It is."

"What if she's a criminal, Eleonore? Have you considered that? What if something's really wrong with her?"

Beau's wife looked down and pushed her toaster back against the wall on the counter. She frowned. Now, she put the sugar pot into the cabinet above her and studied the granules on her plump hand and licked a fat finger.

"Criminal?" she asked.

"I want to get the police. We'll just say we found her the way we did, Eleonore, and get her where she needs to go."

"Is that how the parable went? I don't remember that part of the story." And she loosened the knot of the scarf over her head and led down that no-color hair. It almost touched the ground, and she strung it over her shoulder so that its length was no hinderance in her movement.[1]

"Well, what if she needs attention. Medical attention. She's hurt, badly."

"She's hurt. Yes. I think she'll be fine."

"Maybe, she's been kidnapped and needs us to contact the authorities."

____

[1] Such long hair is not particularly a characteristic of Mormons, especially not in Eleonore's case, as she had lived so isolated for so long.

But Eleonore wouldn't respond to him. And her husband went on. He balked. He frantically bumbled through a string of worst-case scenarios that were all greatly exaggerated and ridiculous.

She could see in his eye the embarrassment of his having become so emotional. There were drops of sweat in his brow. A vein pulsed in his forehead, and he clenched the thick wrist of his other arm as he spoke in desperate pleas for her to cooperate, to not keep the thing which they'd found on the road and brought into the house.

Finally, he said,

"We don't know anything about her, Eleonore, not one thing! What if she's a murderer? I'm leaving tomorrow. You know that."

"She is no such thing, Beau Smith. You should be ashamed of yourself talking about someone like that, and yes, I do know that you are leaving tomorrow. All the more reason, you've nothing to be concerned about with the poor child. There'll be no more talk about this. You won't be back until spring or early summer. She'll be gone and better for it, and we can be sure we did what was right."

A silence inhabited the living room with them. Beau looked down. He swung a foot lightly and side-to-side, balancing himself on the mantel. It was her place. The house belonged Eleonore, and even though things were cordial between them, this was the most communication they'd had in years. This was the most emotion he'd ever shown his wife.

"Now," she said sitting down on the love seat and reached over with pudgy fingers to pick a butterscotch candy out of the crystal glass candy tray on the coffee table. She pinched the ends of the wrapper and pulled them apart so that the yellow disk spun between her fingers and put the piece of candy onto her tongue, "We've got some biscuit and roast from yesterday, if you're hungry. I'm happy to heat some up for you."

The sad husband sat down on the far couch and looked at his hands and his knees and said,

"No, ma'am, I don't reckon I am very hungry at all."

"Let's get to bed, then. You've got an early day, and it's best we sleep."

AND AT NIGHT, untouched in the bed next to the boy she married all those years ago—only now he was fatter and older, a man and she respected him less—the heaviness of her thoughts from the drive returned to her. Some of the harder times she'd had with her self-esteem over the whole marriage came to her in the black bedroom. It was quiet. But he snored next to her and faced away. She could see his back.

He always faced away. And the gift she'd saved for their marriage now rotted in the bed with them, a beautiful blessing become a curse, and she choked for fear that the rest of her life would remain as loveless and touchless as it was in that dark moment, as it had been for the last two decades with her husband. But now, in the warm flickering of images and thoughts between her life and sleep where there was so much despair, something else formed itself in her imagination. It was a strange thing protruding into her mind. An odd vision which she could not forget and which caused a terrible turning in her chest. It was the way the injured girl's legs looked like men's legs and the hair and the warm, rancid breath—the tattoos and the bird bone skull thing around her neck. And now, as she drifted and slept, the grievous wound of her humiliating loneliness—with which she was so familiar—was not. The woman was.

Now, Eleonore's breathing slowed. Her face softened. She slept.

AFTER A WORDLESS MORNING of scowls and no eye contact from the hare-lipped Beau to whom Eleonore was legally married, the man got into his truck and left. Now, Eleonore cracked the door of the side room to check in on the girl in the bed. It was colder in there. Her breath kept the slow, warm rhythm of healing in the tangle of covers and pillows on the bed. In the kitchen, a teapot hissed. Eleonore poured herself a cup and stirred several spoonsful of sugar into it and drank it.

The sun came up over the mountain. And Eleonore drained the tub and filled it again with warm water and let the dirty clothes soak. A dusting of fine, white snow had covered her world during the night—the world that existed hidden from the rest of creation as far as she was concerned, that mountain valley farm and its animals and the small chimneyed house she kept in the midst of the adjacent barns which stored her feed and animals—and the snow kicked up in small swirls as the wind blew. She tracked through it to the barn.

The stocky woman dropped a flake of alfalfa in the wooden trough at the back of the barn, and the three cows mooed and lifted their heads and moved toward her. It was cold. And she blew on her hands. For a moment, she stopped and pushed her thumb into the ratty wood of the stall door where the horse she'd had for 12 years—and which had died that fall—had begun to crib some years prior. He'd gotten older. And though she never had a scale to weigh herself, she knew she was too heavy to make the horse carry her, especially toward the end.

She tossed corn into the chicken coop from a bucket and carried firewood back inside, where she stoked the coals and warmed herself. That pair of red high-top shoes which she'd pulled from the strange woman's feet the night before were wet and, now, steaming by the fire, and Eleonore read the white lettering which said NIKE and pushed up her bottom lip in confusion. And she sat to hold the worn leather of the book she studied every morning. She prayed for her marriage. She prayed for Beau. She prayed for the animals and the hurt thing sleeping under the covers of the side room bed.

Eleonore checked on the girl still sleeping in the room and set the table with a pan of biscuits and a plate of bacon from the last pig she'd slaughtered and butchered all by herself. It was enough for two or three. Though no one joined her, the food was gone when she stood from the table. After that, she sipped a cup of sweet tea and was, soon, filling and draining the tub and moving the clothes around in the water with a stick, until the they were clean enough to handle. Eleonore knelt over the tub. She bit her lip and scrubbed those clothes clean.

Now, she walked out to the area of fenced mud and hay and threw scraps of trash and some feed for the growing pigs. Again, inside, she stoked her fire and sat to study—this time including her old King James bible and The Doctrines and Covenants for cross reference. She unwrapped a candy from the glass plate on her coffee table and put it in her mouth and prayed for strength and the health of the lost girl—the one she'd recovered the night before and whose clothes were hanging by the fire. And before dinner she chopped some firewood and milked her milk cow. It was her intention to make mashed potatoes and green beans to go with the pork chops she'd thawed that afternoon and, most importantly, to share it with the girl, who had not shown any sign of herself outside of sleeping in the bed, at least not yet.

But as the pork chops crackled and Elenore passed the back of her wrist over her brow from the effort of mashing those potatoes, a human noise came from the bedroom. It was hard to hear with the clanging and sizzling of the kitchen and the door of the bedroom closed, but Eleonore hurried to the girl who sat up in the bed with creases in her face and a frown. The black hair had been pushed to one side in a tangle of curls. The girl moaned. And Eleonore spoke softly to her, saying,

"Good morning, or uh, good, um, good aft-good evening." Eleonore stuttered.

She received no response and went on, asking,

"You want some aspirin? You've got a few booboos," and reached out to touch the girl's shoulder. There was a bluing bump on the forehead. The girl looked at her bandaged hand and brushed her fingertips over a half-closed, swollen eye and winced. Her body tensed in a single sob, and tears welled. They hung from her nose and chin, and Eleonore watched with great pity the distress of the feeble being before her.

"Sit back on the bed, Victoria."

The girl straightened her back and leaned against the headboard. She lay on her pillows, and Eleonore stood over her, saying,

"Maybe getting out of bed would be good for you. Can you?"

A slight shrug.

"Want to try?" Eleonore spoke the way she would have spoken to a child.

A slight nod.

"Okay, come on."

But when the girl swung her one swollen ankle out from under the sheet and hung it from the bed, there was no attempt. And Eleonore went on, saying,

"Oh, now, look at that. Your ankle is in bad shape. Let's see if you can walk with me but try to keep your weight off of it. Okay. Let's go."

Eleonore lifted the girl. And they made it to the living room with lots of grunting and a short yell of pain and the girl falling onto the couch across from the fire. She lay down, again. She looked confused, and Eleonore said,

"I made dinner. Are you hungry?"

The girl held her jaw and opened it, as if testing it, and nodded.

"Okay, let's try some mashed potatoes, how's that sound? And let me get you some aspirin."

The pill bottle rattled from the kitchen cabinet. A silent glass of water sweated before the girl on the coffee table. A soft hand held out the two violet-colored tablets to the mannish, grown girl who took them and swallowed them slowly and drank some water and sighed in pain as she placed the glass back onto the table. It was quiet. She would not be getting off of the couch to eat by herself.

An ashy log fell in the fire and sparks spiraled up into the chimney. Eleonore got up to add a log and stoked it, and spoons clanked on glass plates in the kitchen, and now, the squattier woman with the red tones in her skin and scarf-wrapped head sat. She propped up the younger woman's head in her own lap. She fed the soft white meal to the girl on the couch. It was slow. And the girl visibly struggled to move her jaw or close it well enough to swallow the food. Her breath stunk. Eleonore held the glass to her lips and let her drink milk and fed her again and let her drink, and finally, the girl slept. She nuzzled Eleonore's fat thigh and drooled on the skirt of her dress. And Elenore played with the black curls of hair and rubbed the knotty braid hidden in it as if it were a charm made from a rabbit's foot. A smile was on the farm woman's face.

ELEONORE SAT STILL for hours. She let the girl sleep, and as the clock in the hallway chimed two o'clock in the morning, she stood slowly and made another bed for the girl on the couch with covers and pillows and tucked her patient into bed.

Then, Eleonore dressed in her gown and slept in her own room. It was much the same for the following few days. Chores were done. The house was kept. The girl—whom Eleonore addressed as Victoria several times each morning and evening and any time she was awake— said nothing. Her big brown eyes looked out of her skull and watched

Eleonore. The frail figure smiled and ate more. And on the morning following that third day, Eleonore came out of her room rubbing her eye and startled to find the strange girl sitting up on the couch and smiling, as one miraculously recovered, so that it spooked Eleonore.

"You're awake?"

"Yes. I am. Thank you."

"Would you like breakfast?" Eleonore asked and cleared her throat.

"Please," her voice was deeper than most women's.

"Well, let me get it started."

And once the table had been set, Eleonore carried the skinny woman over to it. It was quiet. They ate slowly, not saying much, but from time to time, looking up to study each other, and most of what had been placed on the girl's plate remained. Eleonore had cleaned hers and reached over for more sausage and asked,

"Are you full, Victoria?"

"Oh...I thought I was dreaming!"

"Dreaming what?"

"That you were calling me Victoria."

"Isn't that your name?"

There was a restrained laugh from the young woman as she looked up at Eleonore, saying,

"No. It's not my name."

"It was on your underwear."

"My underwear?"

"Yes. It said something about Victoria's Secret."

"And what did you think my secret was?"

"I don't know."

And now, the boyish younger woman squirmed in her seat looking down into her lap and studying what she saw and asked,

"Do you make your own underwear?"

"Do I...? Yes. I sew all of my clothes." Eleonore said.

"You must have let me wear yours, then," she laughed.

Eleonore blushed.

The other girl went on, laughing and saying,

"Victoria's Secret is a store in Palo Alto. They opened last year, I think. A friend turned me onto them. They make expensive stuff. You might like it..."

"Oh, no," Eleonore's ears and cheeks burned red.

"Ah. No. I'm just kidding. It's okay. But not my style..."

"Not your style?"

"No."

"I don't understand."

"Don't worry about it. We'll just keep it a secret for now." The girl smiled and touched her hair.

"Secret? Okay."

"What's your name? Here, you've... you've...um. I

don't even know your name."

"Eleonore."

The girl put out her thin fingers and waited for the small handshake that followed and said,

"They call me Bird or Birdy."

"Bird or Birdy..." Eleonore put a curled finger to her chin. "Is that short for something?"

"Is it short for something?"

Elenore nodded and picked up a piece of sausage and held it between her teeth before slowly chewing.

"Uh... it's, um. It's short for Bernadette."

"Bernadette. Bernadette. I like that. I really do."

"Call me Bird, please," she squirmed in her chair and touched her chin to the table.

"Okay, Bird."

"Okay, Eleonore." The girl laughed harder this time, but the movement made her wince and suck air through her teeth.

ELEONORE CLEANED THE TABLE and washed the dishes and boiled tea and poured two cups. She put several spoonsful of sugar from her sugar jar into her cup and asked the girl—whom she now called Bird—if she wanted any.

"I like my tea and coffee black, Eleonore. But, since you're offering, I'll take one."

And a lump of sugar was spooned into her cup and stirred. Eleonore handed it off to the woman, noticing the brush of fingertips on her own knuckles. She looked up quickly into the face, which was smiling and calm, and swallowed, hesitating to speak,

"I wish I was like you. I can't help but add too much sugar to everything."

"What's the problem with too much sugar?"

"This…" Eleonore stood at the table and showed her palms to Bird and turned slightly showing her belly and fatter frame.

"What's that?"

"I'm fat. Don't you see?"

"I think you're beautiful," Bird said. It was frank, and she did it while looking into Eleonore's eyes.

Elenore blushed and fumbled for a response, and her heart beat so that she felt weak. It was an unexpected response. No one had ever said such a thing to her in her entire life. And she mumbled the words,

"Thank you."

"It's true."

And Eleonore helped Bird back onto the couch and excused herself as she did chores around the property. Her cheeks were flush. Her ears seemed to be burning.

DAYS PASSED, weeks too. Then, a month had come and gone. And Bird grew in strength. She could walk, now, though it was lanky and awkward when she did, as it had been for the many years before then. But the limp was less. And the wounds which had long since lost their bandages turned into shrinking black scabs which were small and smaller and then mostly nothing but smooth and milky shadows of themselves in the places where they had once been, scars in her olive skin.

The women made small talk. There was never a question about what had happened to Bird that night Eleonore and Beau found her. It never came up. Bird never wanted it to, and in truth, neither did Eleonore. So, the women offered each other friendly, superficial banter while Eleonore worked on whatever chores needed to be done to avoid it. And they spent time together. They walked the property blanketed it in snow and stared at the sky and laughed at the animals or carried firewood into the house by the armful.

At night, Eleonore pulled the stiff, aching woman's boots tenderly from her feet and cooked and cleaned and made her bed for her. Eleonore had nursed Bird. Now, she served her. Bird was the first person who had ever asked Eleonore much of anything about herself. And Bird was the first person to whom Eleonore had revealed her thoughts, had revealed herself. There were long talks at night by the fire and eye contact, looks of knowing and understanding and concern for one another. They were friends.

For the fatter, country woman, it was not only her Christian duty to help the recovering Bird in material or physical ways but also in spiritual. And so, Eleonore would read the scriptures out of her King James Bible and the Book of Mormon and told—as a proof for the authenticity and authority of her holy books—the miracle of the gulls, how a deadly plague of locusts had descended on Utah when the earlier Mormon pioneers had first come to the land and grown their crops.

In the account, the vermin would have eaten up all the food and left thousands of men, women and children dead. Eleonore was excited to tell it. Most everyone she knew in her entire life already knew it, and the thought of sharing with someone for the first time left her standing up in the living room and gesturing with her excited hands about how,

"The gulls had come out of nowhere, after the men and women saw how the crickets were devouring the crop. They were panicked. So, they prayed to God, just the same as anyone of us can do. And out of nowhere here come these birds, Bird..." Eleonore smiled and laughed and said, "Bird. I'm telling stories about birds and look at your name."

Both women laughed, Eleonore heartily, Bird politely.

Soon, Eleonore went on in the firelight. She said,

"But it wasn't just any kind of regular birds coming to eat regular locusts. No. It wasn't a thing like that at all. It was a miracle. The crickets had swarmed in such a way that no matter what flock of gulls had come into the settlement, there was no chance. There were too many, Bird. But the gulls ate like they were starving. They ate every bug in sight, and when they were too full, when they just couldn't possibly eat another one without exploding themselves, the birds drank water and vomited up the creatures and ate more and more for weeks, until the crop was saved. It was a miracle, Bird, a miracle of God."[1]

But there wasn't much response from Bird. The logs popped in the fire place. And after some time, Bird asked,

"Did I ever tell you about...? Nah. I never did. There's no way I told you."

"Tell me what?"

"About the time I was starving in fall somewhere on the east coast and me and my friend were down at the park. We were so hungry, Eleonore. We were so, so hungry. And well, there's usually ducks in the park, you know? But not this park, not this night. Nope. This park we were in, well, it had chickens."

"Chickens?"

"Chickens. Like this..." Bird clucked and moved

---

[1] This is a common history shared by Mormons as proof that they were ordained by God to settle Utah. Much of it is supported by uncontroversial facts about the gulls which did live there at that time and the plague of insects.

her neck and head, imitating a chicken in her seat. "And, look, they were the scrawniest, sorriest looking chickens you ever saw, Eleonore. I swear. And so, me and my girlfriend have this fishing line and a hook and a piece of bread and we throw it out into the park and get a bite and pull it back to us. We had a chicken, and we rung its neck."

"To eat it?"

"To eat it? Of course, to eat it! What else would we do?"

"I don't know. That's what I do when I ring their necks."

"Right. And so, we take it back to this van she has parked by this old bridge and we start a fire in an old barrel. But neither of us knows how to skin a chicken. So, we're like this..." Bird did an absurd pantomime of herself trying to puck each and every feather from the chicken's skin. "And then, when we finally get it skinned, then we have to cut it up and get the meat, you know? But when we do and we finally cook it in a pan on the fire, it eats like a piece of rubber off our shoes. The meat was like eating a rubber spatula."

The pair laughed long and hard. Soon, one was on the ground banging her fist on the rug and the other was laying back on the couch, holding her chest and vibrating with such intense laughter that no sound came out of her. And as the fire died down and the room grew cold, they were yawning and stretching, and Eleonore went to make sure Bird's bed was ready and watched her get into it and told her good night.

NOW, THERE WAS ONE THING which had come to Eleonore's attention. And she couldn't place the exact moment that she'd realized it or begun to wonder about it, but now, she found herself silently staring through the windows in the early morning or late night when Bird was asleep or in the bathroom. She was tensing the muscles in her face. She was questioning something about Bird.

Throughout all the conversations they'd had, in all the talk about her life which Bird had shared with Eleonore, there was no mention of a man. It wasn't as if Eleonore had ever mentioned Beau to Bird, but she did have a ring. There was no need to mention him. And perhaps, less than the absence of men in her stories, it was the regular mention of this or that "girlfriend" which caught Eleonore's attention.

In Eleonore's antiquated world and among her reserved, Mormon people, a girlfriend—at least in the sense of a girl having a girlfriend—was a friend who was a girl. Lots of girls had girlfriends, not that she had any girlfriends growing up or friends at all. It simply was what such speech meant when she heard it. But with Bird, the way this gaunt stranger used the term in conjunction with her masculine manner and strange appearance—it seemed to Eleonore—the word might mean something else entirely.

Eleonore had heard of such things.

Eleonore might not have referred to Bird has having vile affections. Though, her bible did. For she thought the words to be too harsh, especially since she cared—after those weeks together—much for the virile young lady. It was something she thought about once or twice and then more and more, until there were certain interactions between them that caused Eleonore to become distressed about herself and the girl and the true nature of their friendship.

Was Bird a lesby?[1]

____

[1] Being so sheltered from the world and isolated in her life,

A strange thing happened when the plump country woman knelt at the feet of her new gangly friend and untied her boots. There was a joy in it for Eleonore, to give herself up in some way to the woman and kneel in service and make herself vulnerable, as a wife might for her husband. In the plainest sense—of which Eleonore was cognizant—serving the other woman that way was what Eleonore had always wanted, a fulfillment of her femininity, her marital duties.

Then, when Bird sighed with relief and leaned back on the couch, Eleonore would smile and let the warmth from her chest flush into her ears and cheeks. But it was when she looked up to see the woman and thought of Beau that she was sad, again. It fulfilled her one way. But it also hurt her,

---

Eleonore had only heard the word "lesbian" a few times and could not quite remember it correctly.

because Bird was a woman and so was Eleonore. Beau was her husband, and it was with him that she had desired these things. Bird was no man. And she was not her husband.

Eleonore pushed it away from her mind. She didn't think about it, at least as much she could avoid the thoughts about Bird in that way. There were thoughts she did cling to in order to cleanse herself from the dirty feelings she had about Bird's boyishness and strangeness and her own confusion about all of it.

It would never be.

But at night, when she was alone—some weeks after she'd begun to wonder about such things and realized the way she'd begun to treat Bird as a sort of husband, if only on the most superficial levels—a powerful memory entered her mind. It shook her. She fell to the bed, flush in the face with short, shallow breaths. Her heart raced. She gripped the sheets weakly and trembled. The memory had been conveniently misplaced for some time, but now, it returned.

And it could not be ignored.

HER YEARS ON THE FARM HAD BEEN HARD. And it was in the fourth year of marriage to her mostly absent husband, her third on the property. Beau was back at home for a month. His stay was as unaffectionate and smileless as any other she'd endured thus far or would for the years to come. And he was set to leave the morning before their anniversary—which would fall on a Saturday that year—but he never mentioned it.

All he'd asked her was where he might find his socks and if she wanted him to take the truck into town to fill up the barrels for the petroleum store in the barn and get some feed for the animals with the trailer—which she did want and which he did for her—and,

"Eleonore," he asked, "How many calves should we get this year? Won't we have to sell a few, if we keep going? There isn't much room to keep the meat, anymore."

The next morning, he left while it was dark and she was still moving quietly in the warm bed, younger and fitter and readier, then, to bear children than she ever had been or ever would be. It was impossible to get up and moving that morning. He was gone, again. She was slow and almost moaned in pain and lay under the covers in the dark with an empty stomach until the evening and cried.

And the day after he was gone—on the day of their anniversary—pollen and milkweed floated in the air. Eleonore was all by herself, again, on that property and cleaning the horse's stall and fell to her hands and knees. She bawled. The animals watched. And she bawled and shook and moaned.

Snot hung from her nose. Her face was warm and stick and slimy, and more tears fell. It went on like that for hours, until her body hurt and the muscles in her back cramped.

Pathetically, the woman crawled to a bale of hay and knelt on her work dress and apron. Eleonore was folding her hands in prayer. She was biting her wrist as she cried and stopped and whispered the words, like a pitiful child,

"Dear God... I know I haven't been the best of children, but I have tried. And it's hard down here for me, dear Father. My husband... well, you know," at the mention of her husband, Eleonore shook and broke into wordless bawling for some moments and recomposed herself and bawled again and stopped and spoke, more loudly than before, "My Father in Heaven,

please, please help me. Show me a sign that I'll get through this, please, anything. Give me a sign. Anything at all, Father. Anything at all!"

Immediately, something soft and small thudded against the dusty earth outside of the barn where she could see. It was dark and frizzled and moving. Now, it chirped, once, twice, three times and was pathetic, much as she was in that moment.

She stood over it and studied it and kicked at the larger of two grey cats whose name was Tristan and which had been on the property before she purchased it. She picked the tiny bird up and pressed it to her bosom and looked up. There were no nests in the trusses of the barn's roof or in any other place from which it might have fallen. There was no mother circling the birdling, screeching and squawking in its motherly despair from the branches of any nearby tree. But high above her head—

though the sun was blinding—Eleonore saw something make a few circles against the blue sky and fly towards the east. The farm woman guessed that, somehow, the tiny bird had been picked up and dropped from the talons of the hawk to be left rent and writhing and dying of its wounds in the dust at her feet.

Ravens had carried pieces of bread to the waning Elijah in the bible and fed him as he lay in despair in his cave. Noah released a dove from the ark and knew that it was soon time for him and his family to descend from their boat when the dove carried a small olive branch back to him. And there were the many and freakish multitudes of gulls which did save her ancestors in the very land where she herself had grown up.

And as she had prayed to God for a sign, this bird did fall from the sky.

The message—which the birdling carried to Eleonore from her God—shifted its form in the woman's mind. At first, the creature was a symbol of herself in desperation and crying out to be helped. And soon, the thing represented her marriage. It was her duty to trust God to repair what seemed irreparable, just as the bird had to trust her, trust that she was helping the little animal heal up and live from what would have been otherwise mortal wounds. God's ways are not our ways, she would tell herself at night when set her bible down and fed the little bird by the fire.

And as the healing progressed and the bird grew and was bouncing around the porch and squawking and had a great personality, Eleonore drew strength. She had hope in her God. She knew her marriage could and would be saved if she remained faithful, but at other times, she doubted and cried and was—on a certain afternoon in late winter—watching the bird and talking to herself and to her God in her mind, silently.

On that afternoon, Eleonore was distressed. The bird had hopped from the cover of the patio and flapped its wings up into the branches of a tree next to the chicken coup where it lodged and had been for several days. It confused her. Now, she was full of dread and disbelief that, even if God was faithful, Beau would ever be the man she needed him to be. She knew that her husband did not lover her, and—so resigned to that fate—she asked God if, perhaps, there were some other way.

Divorce was no option. But God might take him from her in an accident at work in the Philippines or whatever island on whatever coast he worked next. Her cheeks blushed with embarrassment at her imaginations of such things. And then, it occurred to her that she would still be without a husband, if Beau should perish, and wondered if she would ever find someone to love her, even if it were, somehow, not Beau—not her husband but some other.

Eleonore felt very unlovable and pondered her life and forgot her previous thoughts. Soon, she looked out at the bird and asked,

"Tell me, please. Will I... Will I ever know love? Will I have love in my life?"

Which the raven seemed to hear and to which it responded with three squawks, sounds Eleonore heard as clear human speech, saying,

"Yes. You will." And she asked again. Again, the three sounds came to her from the bird in the tree, saying, "Yes. You will."

In the days that followed, Eleonore's faith in God to restore her marriage to Beau returned. Yet, she occasionally stepped out into the yard or patio or called out from the barn,

"Are you sure?" and the bird responded just as it had the first two times.

She knew it was God speaking to her. Eleonore knew that it was so. But one morning, she woke up turning on her mattress, panicked by a sudden realization: that she had never asked the bird about whether her happiness would come from Beau or not, and as she stepped out to look for the raven in the birch tree by the chickens, there was nothing. He was gone. And he never returned.

The years passed. And nothing ever happened to Beau. So it was, in her mind—the thing which she had received from the bird—a promise from God for Beau's heart to be turned towards her, once and for all, for him to burn passionately toward her and to know her in the way she had always dreamt. Many late afternoons, while the cows audibly chewed their hay and the horse crunched oats in his bucket, Eleonore sat on the haybale and smiled and looked up at the trusses of the barn, trusting and knowing that God had heard her. She knew beyond knowing that God had promised her love. Beau would be a good husband to her, someday.

BUT NOW, AS SHE MOVED UNDER HER COVERS, alone in her room, the whole of that memory and God's promise came back to her. It was not the promise or the memory, themselves, which left her back and legs tensed in bed, which hardened the muscles in her neck and left her teeth grinding as the sun rose that morning. But it was the ambiguity of the nature of that promise which left her restless. There was never an answer concerning Beau specifically from the bird— or from God, in her mind.

And with these fears came other realizations— realizations which compounded her anxiety. Had such things happened in any other instance the way they had recently, her spiritual mind would have made a great deal of what she saw and heard and knew. A bird had come to her in her hour of need, miraculously—in her mind. That bird told her she would know love. And now, a woman who called herself Bird had come just as battered and torn as the tiny animal she'd found that day so many years before.

Each visitor—the tattered birdling which had fallen to the ground in her young and miserable marriage and the bloody woman named Bird—was a pleasant and welcome presence in her life. True companionship had existed between her and the raven. Now, a friendship of laughter and conversation was developing between Eleonore and the woman in her home. As time went on with each of the two visitors, Eleonore's countenance shifted from peaceful to worried, from certain to questioning and confused.

One had fallen from the sky as an answer to her prayers. And it carried a promise. She knew that. Now, though, she wondered with great hesitation and slowness if Bird might—if she could possibly—be the promise.

She couldn't reconcile it in her mind. It couldn't happen. Bird was a woman, just as Eleonore was, however different they may have been. There was no such thing for the religious and lonely wife of Beau Smith. Yet, so much lined up in her mind. There were so many questions, now. She wondered how it had all escaped her before that moment, how she'd forgotten about the birdling, how she'd forgotten the hope she had to finally find love.

Alone in her bed—instead of sleeping—she imagined herself in such awkward scenarios with Bird and shook her head and laughed at how ridiculous it all seemed. It could not be. But maybe it was. She wondered if women could really love women, the way men did. It might be so but not for her. Women did. She knew that. The bible said so, and if anyone looked like they might, it was Bird.

Eleonore bit her nails. She sniffed in the blue daylight coming through the window in her bedroom. She asked herself if it could be, if it was possible. She had to admit that it was, however much she hated it, however much it worried her.

Eleonore had heard of such things.

NOW, THERE WERE SMALL TOUCHES— apparently accidental—a brush of the hairs on their wrists as they passed one another in the kitchen or the side of Bird's thigh pressed against Eleonore's as she helped with wash. The small touches turned into unnecessary hands placed on Eleonore's knee or shoulder or the small of the back when they talked or faced the stove as pots boiled.

They had long conversations, too. And it was during these moments with Bird that Eleonore relaxed. There was nothing to consider. There was no reason to worry. She smiled and leaned forward and listened when Bird spoke about her younger life in Mexico City and her time on the coast outside of places like Acapulco or inland in San Miguel de Allende.

Soon, Bird told Eleonore that she'd had a dream. And in that dream, it was revealed to her that the charm around her neck should be given to Eleonore and that the talisman—though she wouldn't call it that to Eleonore—had been given to her some years prior by another woman who had worn it and who, also, had a dream to give it to Bird.

There was a sweet moment of ritual as Bird stood behind Eleonore and untied it from her own neck and placed it around Eleonore's. Bird's fingers brushed Eleonore's neck as she tied the leather. Once the gift had been given and the women stood to go to their respective rooms for sleep, Bird hugged a tense and resistant Eleonore who ended the embrace and said,

"Good night!" and shut her bedroom door.

The fire was dying, and a few black logs smoked and hissed quietly. Bird stood and nodded slightly with her hands on her hips. She was smiling in the dark.

Mornings and afternoons after that night, the amulet could be found between Eleonore's fingers when she was alone in the barn—or on the backside of the house or in the kitchen cooking for her companion. It was calming. It helped the round conservative woman quit chewing the fingernails on her fat pink fingers.

Eleonore never took the necklace off of her neck. She woke up with it and stood in the mirror and studied the cracks in the bird bone skull and a bubble in the amber and smiled. There was peace, again. She was comfortable with the visiting woman. Eleonore was often smiling.

AND IN FEBRUARY, after milking the cow and carrying in firewood, they cooked and ate dinner. Soon, the women sat in the living room. The evening was dark and cold, and Eleonore asked about Bird's tattoos.

"Is that why you got them?"

"What do you mean?"

"You got them, because you're Bird."

"Ohhh... yes."

"They're pretty."

"Aw. Thank you."

"I've not ever gotten one, myself."

"Yeah. I'm not surprised," Bird laughed.

"We don't get them."

"What do you mean? Mormons?"

"Yes. Mormons. But we're not supposed to drink tea either," Eleonore made a face, squeezing her eyes shut.

"My first love..." the black-haired woman trailed off, looking from the sides of her eyes at Eleonore leaning forward in her seat to hear the rest. Bird shook her head. "Nooo... Never mind."

But Eleonore insisted,

"Yes? Your first love! Please, tell me."

Bird groaned dramatically and said,

"She was a Christian."

"Oh, Mormon?"

"No. Pentecostal."

"I don't know much about it, but I know we're different. At least, that's what I've heard."

"Yes."

"And?"

"And what?"

"Your first love. You were going to tell me about your first love."

Bird looked jokingly around the room and back at Eleonore and said,

"Did I say that?"

The fatter woman nodded.

"Okay. Fine. I did. Are you ready?"

"Yes."

"Okay, then. I'm going to tell you, but we have to start at the beginning, how I got into the situation that led me to her in the first place."

"Her?" Eleonore asked and swallowed, her eyes gleaming and big.

"Do you want me to tell the story or not, Eleonore?"

"Sure. I just... I just... go on. Forgive me."

And she spoke quietly to the round face of the shorter, fatter woman.

Bird told of her early life as the only child of an impoverished couple that lived on a cursed bog of a property in the rural lands of coastal Maine. Her father drowned in drink, the grandson of Irish immigrants. Her mother—a dark eyed islander of some sort who spoke some English and mostly pigeon—had been a circus performer and had fallen from the top of a crowded tent and was left permanently disfigured by the fall. By unlikely happenstance, Bird's mother met and married Bird's father and conceived the girl, but as the thin, black-haired girl grew, her mother's reputation of being a harlot and unfaithful to her husband in the small rural town preceded the family entire.

By the time Bird turned eight years old, her mother had moved into an ancient looking house and gotten the same strange, androgenous haircut as the other bug-eyed men and women with whom she shared the communal living space. They called themselves, "Howardites." Their leader was a leering and long faced theologian known as "The Doctor Howard," and by the time Bird was ten, her mother moved west with that bizarre collection of human beings and was never heard from or seen, again.

"I have hated religion, ever since, Eleonore."

"It's okay. Don't..." and before she could say anything else, Bird continued, telling of how her old man lay in drink around the house. He was, himself, dying, and she turned 13 starving and alone in that squalor. And she left. Bird went on telling of the nights in the freezing streets of Boston and New York City and

Pittsburgh where she was adopted by a transient family of big-nosed and yellow skinned people.

"I was with them for about a year, by the time they wanted me to marry one of their nephews or cousins or someone." Now, Bird stood holding the mantlepiece and leaning toward the fire and staring down into it.

"They wanted you to marry someone? Like an arranged marriage?"

Bird nodded silently. The orange glow of the fire pulsed on her face as Eleonore gazed carefully at the lanky woman.

"Sometimes, we have those. My mom wanted my sister to marry someone, but she left home."

"What happened to her?"

"She died in a car accident in California."

"Oh, no. I'm sorry."

"It's okay. I didn't know her. I just know the story."

"Hmmm…"

"Anyway, go on."

"Are you sure you want to hear this?"

Eleonore twiddled the necklace Bird had given her and dragged her fingertip over the edge of the arrowhead. She sat and stared at the woman— who was standing and telling the story—and rubbed the smooth ball of amber and nodded,

"Yes. I'm sure." Her knees pointed toward the woman at the fire place.

"Okay, then… Where was I?"

"The arranged marriage."

"Oh, yeah. His name was Rami."

"Rami?"

"Yeah. He was the ugliest thing I'd ever seen in my life, and the family talked about it. They loved me, you know? I loved them, too. They'd been so good to me. And, anyway, they put me in a dress that was way too tight and this crazy headdress looking thing or whatever it was. I don't know. And we had a ceremony. There was dancing and yipping around a huge bonfire on the beach in North Carolina, and I got drunk."

"Drunk?"

"Yeah. Drunk. I might tell you about being drunk, one day, too."

"Okay?"

"And that night... that night... our first night together married, I knew..."

"Knew what?" Eleonore leaned forward and to the side in her seat. She rubbed one knee slowly and listened and forgot to breathe, recalling her own marriage and that first night, so much pain, so much shame. She placed her hand over her heart and stared, listening.

"That it wasn't that way for me, Eleonore."

"What do you mean?"

"What do you think I mean?"

Eleonore opened her mouth, but no sound came out, and Bird continued, telling how she waited till the hours before the sun came up and her new husband was snoring loudly in their RV—what was supposed to be the beginning of their life together in their new home and said,

"Then, I left. I fled in the dawn and made it to Asheville, North Carolina, and I was so young. Still a child, and I had a few hundred dollars that I'd taken, and I got men to buy me beer and drank it all away and cut my hair off so boys wouldn't like me and hitchhiked with strangers up into the hill country of Appalachia and was over in Tennessee when a local pastor found me outside of a gas station, and I was drunk."

The pastor and his wife— who were both old in age and also without any children who weren't already grown and gone from the home—adopted her as a sort of charity case, and he preached, most nights of the week, in a north facing building that was little more than the temporary husk of a whitewashed chapel, like some roving revival tent where men stomped their clogs so that the earth itself shook and clapped their hands and waved sweaty handkerchiefs in ecstatic rapture.

Some fell on the floor and writhed and shouted as if in pain. And on certain nights of the week, the men would carry out a wooden box like a coffin in the procession of some heretical set. They would lay it down in the midst of the congregation and would open it. There were, inside, a number of snakes thumping around, and some of the men, as they felt led, would take up the poisonous things and be bit or extract the venom from the vipers' pink fangs and collect it in a small mason jar and hold it up for all to see and drink it to show that it would not hurt them.

"Two men died of it."

"Really?"

"They did, and I was there, you know, just hanging out. The pastor was a nice guy, normal, and he had me working in a rich lady's—a millionaires'—horse barn in the next little town over, about five miles away."

"And you went to a church like that?"

"Well, yeah. But you know, it sounds crazier than it was."

"If they were drinking snake venom, then it's crazy, Bird."

"True. Very true. And it was crazy. Like I told you, before, I hated religion, so I figured it was okay, because religion was crazy to me, in the first place. And anyway, I'd go up and put my head on the altar at the end of Sunday morning services and show them that I was at least trying to become a Christian, even if I hated it. And I carried a bible."

"Why?"

Bird bit a piece of skin on her knuckle and spat it into the flames of the fire burning in the fireplace. She thought and said,

"I was going to school. They let me stay for free. They fed me, even though I was saying I was a vegetarian, which they thought was weird, and they let me eat cereal and oatmeal every morning. I had nowhere else to go, though, Eleonore. I was young and scared."

Eleonore nodded,

"Did you learn any of it?"

"Not really. Nothing I can remember, now."

"And?"

"And I think they kind of held me at a distance, like I was a black cat or something. They were always trying to get me to wear girl clothes, and I wouldn't have it. I mean,

sometimes, I would, just to shut 'em up. And so, people knew. At least, I think they whispered behind my back that I liked girls, and they were right about that. Still, though, I didn't like it that they talked or looked at me like they did. And I used to sit behind this woman and her family. Her husband was with her pretty often. She'd had a few kids, and you could see that their marriage was...was... um, well..."

"What?"

"She wasn't happy. It was obvious that she'd been very pretty when she was younger, even though she was young, then, and pretty, but she'd been married and had gotten fatter and didn't have time for herself, I guess. And at first, you could see how she'd try to be sweet to her man when he was with her. And you could see how he pushed her hand away when she reached for him. I can't say what it was, exactly, but he was angry looking or something. He shook his head a lot, you know, like he didn't love her, like she was too fat."

Eleonore tried to slow her breathing and pushed her fingertips into her mouth. She pulled a pillow into her lap and hugged another against her chest as if hiding her own fatness, her own likeness being found in the story Bird told.

Bird cleared her throat and swallowed loudly before speaking,

"So, as the time went on, I just sat there, and I'd see her every Sunday, and she'd look back at me, and I knew. I knew through her eyes that there was so much pain in her about herself, the aching of something amiss in their marriage was communicated to me. You know what I mean?"

There were heavy thumps of heartbeat in Eleonore's throat, now. She was paralyzed by the shame she felt in hearing this story that was her own,

and how—or so she guessed—these same events led to a lesbian love affair between the married woman and Bird. It scared her. It terrified her and pulled her in at the same time.

And she bumbled and muttered the words,

"Um... I don't know, quite, if I do."

"Her husband didn't love her."

"And... and how did you know that?"

Bird looked into Eleonore's eyes and said,

"I just did, Eleonore. I'm a woman like she was, even if I don't like dressing up as one. Her eyes betrayed her loneliness, and something about the way she saw me looking at her, seeing her in it... well, the pastor and his wife took me to their little meetings every night, and every night, the woman was there, too, once she realized I was there with the pastor and his wife every night, and every time she got a chance, that woman was stealing a look, looking back at me looking at her."

Eleonore looked away and asked,

"What about her husband? How old was she?"

"Maybe, 28. He didn't come much, anymore. And one morning, before school, the pastor told me at breakfast I was going to start helping the lady, that same lady, with taking care of her kids, instead of working at the horse barn, and so I went over there after school and sat with her and her kids, and her husband was working in a mine, and when the kids went to sleep, she met me in the living room and I never..." Bird stared off as if she'd come to some great monument in her own mind and was beholding its beauty in awe for some moments before going on.

"Never what?"

"Ah. You don't want to know."

"Sure, I do." Eleonore leaned forward.

"We fell in love," now, Bird turned her back to the fire and grabbed her wrist behind herself, holding her head back and closing her eyes. "We were absolutely in love. She had the whitest, softest skin in the whole world and the blackest hair and the bluest eyes. And somedays, I'd come to her and the kids after school, and the doors would be broken off the hinges around the house. Or there'd be smashed glass on the floor. Sometimes, she'd have a black eye. And when it was dark and the kids went to sleep, I'd tell her about how we could escape as I held her by the fire place, and we made plans to leave."

"How long was it?"

"How long were we like that? Maybe, a month. Maybe, two. I don't remember. It was something so powerful and so strong that time didn't matter, Eleonore, and well... anyway, she had some money. And I did, too."

"What? She was going to leave her kids?"

"I don't know, Eleonore. I don't think we ever talked about it like that."

"Hmm..."

"We made plans to meet at the horse barn in the next town over, where I was working before. And I snuck out of my window at the pastor's house that night and waited in the starry morning by the barn. I waited for my hillbilly woman, but she never came."

"What happened?"

Bird said that a couple of pickups had pulled over on the side of the road in front of the horse barn, and in the back of one was a small band of men. They were wielding pitchforks and torches, and some were loading shotguns and walking towards the barn.

Dogs were barking. The hillbilly woman's husband led them.

"And I knew... I knew she'd told him all about me. I knew she'd turned me in to him to save herself or got cold feet or something, and it hurt. My heart was broken in a way that it will not and can never break again, Eleonore, but I didn't have time for that, then. They had some dogs and were moving quick, so I buried myself in a huge mound of horse dung. I was in fear for my life, Eleonore, from the angry townspeople hunting me like a monster fled to the hills, and I never liked religion, and religion was why they were chasing me in the first place. But that night, that night I called on the name of the Lord, anyway, and begged him to save me from that nightmare, to spare me from that evil."

"I don't like that you were going to take her from her husband, Bird. That's not right."

There was silence in the room. Bird cleared her throat and shifted her weight. She opened her eyes and stared at Eleonore, clenching her hidden teeth and fist—incredulous that such a statement was all the fat farm woman had to say about it. It was another moment, before she spoke to say,

"And what about you?"

"What about me?"

"You're married, aren't you?" Bird pointed at the thin silver band cutting into Eleonore's fat finger.

"Yes. You know that."

"You haven't told me that. I don't see any pictures of him in here, but you have the ring. You act like a married woman, too."

"Act like a married woman? And what does that mean?"

"You're miserable and stuck with someone who doesn't know you or what you want or how to give it to you. Maybe, he doesn't even touch you. Where is he? You don't seem to be too happy about it."

"Beau Smith is a good man," Eleonore choked out, shaking her head spasmodically.

"He's a good man?" Bird drew the words, incredulous and mocking, and gestured, now, as she spoke. "Why don't you have children? A woman like you, don't you want children?"

Elenore stood and looked about, startled, trembling. Soon, she was gazing out into the last hints of daylight and set her gaze upon the barn in the distance and touched her teeth. It was a fidgety few moments. Then, she spoke calmly, saying,

"That's none of your business. I'm sorry for the misunderstanding, here. I'll be going to bed for the night. If you're hungry, you can get whatever you like. Good night, Bird."

Bird reached for the woman as she passed. It

was dark in the house, and now, Eleonore's bedroom door slammed shut. Bird collapsed onto the couch, dejected and shaking her head.

FOR THE NEXT WEEK AND MORE, Eleonore offered little but tight-lipped grunts and an occasional word to Bird about when to eat and the like. It had been their custom to eat at the table together. But now, Eleonore prepared the other woman's dinner or breakfast.

Then, she made excuses about chores that needed to be done so that she wouldn't sit at the table and eat. Sometimes, she split an extra stack of firewood. Sometimes, the farm woman spent time stroking the soft hairs of her small cow. Other times, she sat on the hay in the barn for such long periods of time that Bird would come out and ask,

"What are you doing out here?" in a low voice, the breath from her mouth and nose turning to clouds in the cold.

"Thinking," she would say and pass by the taller, lankier female and look to the ground, so that Bird would laugh at the display of frustration from the chubbier lady.

No longer able to soothe her lately-feeble mind and feelings about Bird and herself with the pleasant conversations they had, Eleonore's perception of the woman turned negative. Bird was not welcome. She was disgusting.

Eleonore wondered if, maybe, she might hate the other woman. The breath was intolerable. Bird didn't bathe as much as she should, either, so that her whole bedroom smelled like old sweat and musty foot. Eleonore scrunched her nose when she thought of the thick yellow toenails on the woman's feet which were attached to that pair of hairy man's legs.

The hideousness of it all lay bare. The vulgar nature of the strange woman was plain to see. It was something Eleonore could not tolerate. And for several days in a row—for the first time in Eleonore's life—she had not opened her Book of Mormon or bible or any of the others. She was sitting in her chair or on her bed, her face drawn in a sneer. She stared at the floor, stared at nothing and shook her head.

In ways, the boyish creature with its terrible breath called Bird became an obsession for Eleonore. For the time, though— those first days after Bird told her story to Eleonore—it was clothed in the flesh of animus and resentment. She was frustrated. It was all she thought about. But as the week drew on and another started, the alienation of Eleonore's mind toward Bird wore her down.

The less they spoke, the more Eleonore found herself wishing they would. She missed that pair of brown eyes looking down into hers. She longed to smile and laugh with her friend, again, even if her friend was unnatural, even if Bird had wounded her and made her so uncomfortable. Eleonore wanted to apologize. But she didn't know how. Those were dark days. It snowed heavily. The light was muted and grey, and Bird stayed up late by herself, sitting in front of the fire with her legs crossed and woke up later every morning. Eleonore stayed in her room or worked silently outside during the daytime.

ELEONORE WOKE LONG BEFORE THE SUN CAME UP. It was the 14th day since Bird told the story of her first love by the fire. A sort of anxious despair had come over Eleonore, and sleeping was harder for her than it had been since the first years of her marriage to Beau. The regular prayer and reading of the scriptures—which she'd maintained so faithfully her entire life—had waned. It was time to commit herself to God, again. It was time to commit herself to mercy and being merciful.

Now, she stood in the quiet kitchen and boiled water and poured herself a cup of tea. She placed her bible and the Book of Mormon on the counter and opened the cabinet and pulled down her sugar pot and reached into it. There was something in it, though, a piece of paper folded into a small square, and she opened it.

It said this:

Dearest E,

I understand that you are mad. I said things I shouldn't have said.

Beau Smith is a fine man. He is your husband. You are his wife.

Who am I to disrespect that? I spoke out of turn and in ignorance.

But now, in the chasm that has opened up between us, I feel as though

My heart is broken. And in the insufferable woe of our separation,

I have come to know one thing. I CANNOT LIVE WITHOUT YOU.

Forever and always,

Your Birdy

Eleonore said nothing of the note. She only pressed it into the corner of her most personal drawer as if it were the seed of something greater being hidden in her heart's chambers. There were smiles, again, between them.

They talked. By evening, they were laughing so hard that Eleonore was wiping tears from her eyes and on her back, rocking on the rug by the couch. And in the small blue light of the following dawn, there was another note.

It said this:

Dearest E,

You never mentioned the note. I know you have it.

And to have your smile, to behold your face the way I did today,

Reaffirms everything I already know. I think you know it, too.

If you want me to stop, put the sugar jar next to the toaster on the counter.

If you want my confession, put it on the kitchen table.

Forever and always,

Your Bird

In the days that followed, Bird stood up in the living room and lengthened her neck—or put her plate in the sink for Eleonore to wash after their meals—to see if the sugar jar was on the table or on the counter. It was nowhere to be seen. But as if in innocent taunting, Eleonore would pull it down from the cabinet and removed its top to offer sugar to Bird whenever they drank tea, showing her that whatever had been placed in it the night before had been removed. Bird shyly reminded the farm woman, every time it happened, that she liked her tea black.

They talked long and often in the firelight.

Eleonore could be seen pulling the gift—that bauble of amber and bone and rock which hung from her neck and which her companion had given her—out from under her collar. She held it. Her fingers played with it carefully when they talked.

Bird talked of horoscopes and astrology and explained to the eagerly listening and leaning Eleonore what it meant to be a Virgo and how that affected relationships with Cancers. Bird pressed her long, thin finger into Eleonore's forehead and spoke of the third eye, the pineal gland. There was mention of chacras and healing.

For several more weeks Bird stood on her toes with a straight back, craning to see where the sugar pot would be every morning. Eleonore had caught herself taking extra time to choose her best and cleanest dresses. She was pushing her hair around in the mirror every morning and throughout the day.

Now, they stood together in the kitchen. It was early in the evening, before eight o'clock. And they'd finished some dinner and sipped their cups of tea. Eleonore was playing with the sugar pot, sliding it around gently with her fingertips across the table and stood slowly and looked down at Bird, who was sitting with her knees spread like a man.

"Good night, Birdy."

"Good night, E," it was the first time they'd used the names, which had only been used by Bird in the secret sugar pot notes she left for Eleonore. Both women were blushing.

And in the morning, Eleonore finally found another note. She stood there in the quiet black, wearing only her slippers and nightgown and pulled it with great joy from the ceramic jar.

It said this:

My love, My beautiful E,

I have loved you. I have always loved you.

It was only that I didn't know you, yet.

But, now, I am yours. You are mine.

There is no life without you.

-Your Birdy

THE DAYS PASSED SLOW AND WARM inside of the house by the fire, as winter howled outside. Those were the last days of February. And thoughts of Beau and his return from his job—which Eleonore knew to be in South Africa—flickered in her mind for a moment. They dissipated as quickly as they'd come. And in a strange way, she'd learned to enjoy the stink of Bird's breath during their slow, soft conversations in the living room. It was familiar. It was the most intimacy she had ever known with anyone.

Still, the notes were a secret, never mentioned between them explicitly but existing as some invisible faith in an expected and coming reality, the advent for which they hoped but which both harbored quietly inside of themselves with fear and trembling, so that their hands—at different times—visibly shook with anticipation and emotion as they interacted or thoughts of the other flooded their minds. And the impassioned notes increased in their fervor.

They said things like:

"I dream of your skin and your lips," or, "I love you beyond all measure, Eleonore," or, "I will marry you," and, "You will be my wife, and I will be your husband. Come to me," and more and more, the phrase reappeared,

"Come to me. Come to me, Eleonore. I love you. I wait for you every night. Please. Come to me."

Such words being strung together were hard to read. They were dangerous. They could mean death, in Eleonore's world, something Bird herself had seen in her own life. Those erotic proclamations simultaneously repulsed Eleonore. Yet somehow, in that repulsion, she found herself captivated by them and by the woman who wrote them to her. Eleonore pressed the small folds of paper to her chest and bounced in glee alone in the still mornings. There were, perhaps eight which expressed so candidly Bird's romantic desires. Most mornings, Eleonore squealed quietly. She smiled and bit her knuckle and pressed the love letters to her chest. But she never did come to Bird.

The days of March dragged on as if never ending. Snow melted. And all the yard turned into a cold and miserable soup of mud and slush. It was this way every year on the old property. It is still, and Eleonore stayed busy—she'd sewn a new dress for herself—while Bird stayed inside, and the farm woman was wearing that black work dress she'd made. It fit her tightly so that she tugged and fidgeted and had asked,

"Bird, how do I look in this dress?" as one desperate to be affirmed.

In the cold and in contrast to the dark color of the fabric, her skin was pink, as she chopped firewood in it one blue afternoon. Bird came out of the house. She was wearing her pants and the red high-top tennis shoes that she'd come into Eleonore's life wearing.

They stood by the barn. One of the cows bellowed lowly and dramatically. The growing calf responded with a noise of its own. Eleonore heaved the maul to split rounds of firewood and stopped and rested on the handle of the maul and asked with a great smile and posing, as if for the other woman,

"What's on your mind, Birdy?"

Bird didn't speak.

She stood staring and thinking and breathing and stared at Eleonore's lips. There was a wall of cracked pine rounds with faces patinaed by age and the lichens that grew on them. For a moment, Bird steadied herself with a hand against the old rounds of firewood. She leaned forward. There was a quiet fumbling of the one's thin, smooth fingers at the backs of the other's soft, pink hand and a hurried press of cold lips and a tooth into dry chin. There was a pause and an adjustment and the warm lung breath of one woman breathed in by the other. Now, there was the tiny clack of tooth against tooth. Eleonore pulled away.

Birdy stood smiling and holding her hands out. Eleonore's mouth hung open. Before any words could be said, the sharp, loud snap of Eleonore's palm against the skin of Bird's cheek echoed back from the rocky hill in the trees behind the barn. A slight trickle of blood ran onto Bird's tongue, and she touched her lip.

Eleonore said, loudly,

"You were wrong for that. You know you were. I'm sorry. I'm going inside, now."

A PAINFUL SEVERING took place that day. There was a break in communication. They lived once more as strangers in the same dwelling. They were never rude, but they were cold and quiet.

The roles, though, had mostly switched.

Now, it was Bird who spent her days in her room. She grunted short answers to Eleonore and lay on the bed and had collected a pair of empty notebooks from the forgotten corners of the house and spent her afternoons on her belly scribbling in them.

And alone in the pink morning light, Eleonore checked her sugar pot. It was without the notes which had been there before. The fat woman slumped at her table. She held her head in her hand and frowned and saw her books—the bible and Book of Mormon—on the table where she had left them some weeks before, on the morning she found the first note.

And one day, Bird asked for a stamp and an envelope. A squinting Eleonore obliged, slowly fetching and handing her the items.

The next morning, when she woke up, she found on the kitchen table under the sugar pot—the table having become its new home—the   sealed envelope and another piece of paper. The black ink and handwriting were Bird's.

It said:

I don't know when you send out mail, but if you go before, I'm awake, please mail this.

Thank you

Upon inspection, Elenore read that it was addressed to another woman in a correctional facility in Florida. The name was Lavonne Sterling. And Eleonore's hands were, immediately, rubbing her thighs and pinching at the fabric of her skirt and clenched, one inside of the other.

Breakfast was not cooked.

She had no appetite, and the flesh around the bones in her arms and legs worked silently with a strange listlessness which she had never known. For a moment, her face contorted as if to cry but did not. She paced. She staggered weakly around the kitchen and living room without a cup of tea nor a glass of water, without changing into her clothes for the day, and in her bedroom, she cried to herself and tore into the envelope and pulled a letter from it.

The letter had, written in Bird's hand, statements about Eleonore. It called her sad. It said she was a fuddy-duddy and the lonely farm woman who didn't know love and never would. Bird expressed herself to this Lavonne Sterling, that she only wished she and Lavonne could be together, again, referring to Lavonne as a real lover. Bird said she missed the woman. She said everything with Eleonore had been a mistake and that she had mixed feelings for the country woman. How could she carry on with someone like Eleonore, someone so square and rigid and unable to love her the way Lavonne and so many other women had. It wouldn't work.

WHEN BIRD STEPPED OUT OF HER BEDROOM to use the bathroom, it was late morning, and the question,

"Who is Lavonne Sterling?" came to her out of the darkness of the living room.

"Eleonore?" Bird rubbed her eye and coughed slightly.

"Who is she?"

"A friend of mine. Is that okay?"

"A friend?" Elenore's voice was loud and shrill and hurt.

"Yes, a friend," Bird shook her head and walked to the bathroom and closed the door and came out, asking, "And what's it to you, anyway?"

"What's it to me?"

"Yeah. Why do you care, huh?"

Eleonore sat down in the dark and looked away. She said nothing and wept until she was moaning and openly waling there in the house. Bird closed the door to her bedroom and smirked silently at the ceiling for some time before she could fall back asleep.

ONCE AGAIN, Eleonore feels herself choking in the dark of her cold bedroom at night and alone. It is as before, only worse, because now, she has tasted the sweetness of being desired. She knows, seemingly for the first time in her life, that someone wants to touch her, to be with her. But she has lost it with only herself to blame. She was a coward.

She struggles to work. She can't eat much. And at night, she is standing up in her room, alone with the lights on and pressing her fingers into her bottom lip and wears her sleeping gown. She thinks of what she's lost. Her heart beats so that her legs are weak, and she holds herself up on the bedpost. Three nights in a row, she stands with her hand on the doorknob working up the nerve to leave her room and go to the woman, but she cannot. She will not step out of her room. She is tormented. She is wrestling with herself.

Finally, sometime in mid-April, Eleonore stands with her one hand on the doorknob, clutching the hem of her nightgown in the other. She shakes her head. She whispers something to herself, telling herself that she can and that she has to do it. It is just after two in the morning.

And the door to Bird's room squeaks as it opens. The room is strangely silent. It is electric in the dark, and Eleonore clutches the coarse white fabric of her nightgown, standing next to the bed.

She is breathing.

She is breathing, as if the air is thin, and now, the lanky and musky woman is stirring under her covers, moving her head and groggily asking,

"Is that you, Eleonore?"

"Yea," Eleonore's throat is dry and useless. She flexes her arms and stands on her toes.

A moment passes.

Again, Bird speaks as one carefully discerning dream from truth,

"You came. You came to me. Is this it?"

Silence.

Eleonore's heart thumps. She is weak and flush.

"Is this what you want, then?" Bird asks.

Eleonore struggles to make words, struggles to breathe. She puts a hand on her hip and lifts her shoulders for one loud breath, before she chokes out one more,

"Yes."

"Gawlee, girl. What took you so long?" Bird lifts the covers.

Warmth and the rank smell of Bird's sweat and sleep rise up from the mattress into Eleonore's face. The necklace Bird had given the fatter woman those weeks before—it seems like years, now—rattles quietly on Eleonore's collar bone as she moves. She touches it. The universe is silent, a dream which contains only this moment and the creature into whose bed she climbs.

And Eleonore is paralyzed. She is unable to breath, unable to move.

Bird drops the covers and makes room and exhales through her nose impatiently. She lifts them up, one more time, and sighs,

"What are you waiting for, then, girly? Come on. Get in."

FIVE YEARS EARLIER, from the bottom bunk of a holding cell in the Clatsop County courthouse, a younger Bird—whose true name was then and always has been Samantha McCool—made a cackling confession of sorts to the gray-haired guard everyone called Birch.

She wore bleached yellow hair at the time. It was more feminine than when she met Eleonore years later. It was much longer and uncombed. Her shoulders were just as square. Her jaw and neck were just as masculine, though thinner. The poor fit of the jailhouse attire made her look rough and criminal.

Samantha McCool spoke with a fake Texas accent, then.

She was the supposed heiress—a niece or perhaps an illegitimate daughter—from a family of Lampasas County cattle barons—using the name Vivian Varon—and had come to mingle among

Astoria's upper-class. After a year in town, she was arrested for embezzlement and identity fraud and various conspiracy charges as well as contributing to the delinquency of a minor. According to her public appointed lawyer, the conspiracy charges would be the thing for which she would be locked up. They were why she would serve time.

"How's Linda?" she asked the guard.

"Linda?"

"Officer Chapman. The one you replaced?"

"Oh, Chapman? You know I don't talk to her."

"How would I know that Birch?"

"You got her fired. Don't talk to fired people when you're not fired. I'm too busy working. I'm here. You probably could figure it out."

"Can you tell her I miss her and need to see her?" The inmate laughed. She was speaking in a heavy New England accent and brushed an eyebrow with her finger and pushed the peroxided hair from her face.

"I don't talk to her. I done told you that. Besides, you had her so wrapped up, she's banned from visiting any jails in the state, ever again. Guards can't have relationships with the inmates. Got a misdemeanor for whatever she was bringing you in here."

"Yeah, well when are they going to put her in here with me? I miss that woman. She really was something."

The old guard fiddled with his nametag that said 'Birch' and studied the inmate and said with suspicious eyes,

"Tell me, how do you do it?"

"Do what Birch?" She said without looking up. The girl was slowly rolling a small cigarette in her crossed-legged lap and pushing her back against the wall. "Roll cigarettes? Or what? I'm not sure what you see me doing in here you gotta ask me how to do it."

"How is it you have them chase you like that? Why are they crazy for you?"

"Oh, you mean that out there?" She laughed.[1]

The girl with the bird tattoos on her chest and arms and stomach licked the gum on her cigarette paper. She pinched the ends of it and looked at the guard.

He said,

"Yeah... all that out there. You had the old Mrs... Miss... what's her name?"

"Her name is Edith, Birch. Edith Stern Bernstein. Worth some 19 million dollars."

---

[1] During the hour which preceded their conversation in the courthouse cell, a terrible commotion had broken out in the inmate's trial. A young blonde girl who was the daughter of the sheriff in the next town had been called to the stand and made to admit that she'd been manipulated by the woman who called herself Vivian Varon and that Vivian Varon was not her name at all but Samantha McCool. The courtroom gasped, being full of common antiquated folks from the surrounding areas. Soon, the prosecutor played a tape on which the young blonde witness and the defendant talked about the late Mr. Bernstein's wife who had been the subject of Samantha McCool's lesbian affections and her grifting. Once the defendant's voice played on the tape, saying, "I don't love her, baby," to the witness, "I don't love her at all. She's noting but an old rag, a hag. She ain't beautiful like you. I don't love her, just want her money. I love you," an old lady shrieked and charged the defendant from the crowd. It was Mrs. Bernstein in disguise, watching incognito. Scorned by the words, she lost her senses and tried to physically hurt the defendant. The judge banged his gavel. Proceedings were finished, until tomorrow.

"And Chapman. Old Linda, you got her all strung up over you, too. How is it so? I don't understand."

"Maybe, Birch, a thing like that isn't for you. Maybe, it's not for you to understand, at all."

"Entertain me. You ain't going nowhere. Me neither. Let's hear it. I mean, look, I've got four sisters and a wife and two daughters of my own. I have aunts and cousins and sisters-in-law. None of them, not one that I have ever heard of, has ever had women."

"What do you want me to say, huh? Maybe, that's cultural. You're black. I'm something else, and the ones I get are white, mostly. Something about them. They seem to have bad marriages, at least the ones I get. That's just the older ones. The younger ones, well... they're easy."

"Oh, so you're racist, too, huh?" The guard was laughing.

"Oh, c'mon. You know I ain't. I'm just telling you what I know," she said in the southern accent she'd used for the last year or so in Astoria. As quickly as she'd broken into it, she broke out of it.

"I know. I know. What about the younger ones, then, huh? Maybe, I can see the older ones with their bad marriages, but still... it seems..."

"Look Birch, I don't really know what to say. I mean, there's some practical stuff. Maybe, some of it's magic."

"Magic?"

"Yeah. Maybe, I'm a witch or something and put the juju on them. I don't know."[1]

"Hmmm..." he pinched his

---

[1] Reportedly, Bird a.k.a. Samantha McCool spent a pair of years living in Mexico where she was used by the leader of a sex cult to groom young girls living there from England and the U.S.

chin. "What about it's practical?"

"Most women...the women I've known and loved and who have fallen for me...those women? Those women are like clocks and horses."

The old guard clapped his hands and stomped a foot on the other side of the bars and fell to the side slowly in laughter, repeating,

"Clocks and horses?"

"Yeah. Clocks and horses. You got a match? Light my cigarette," she asked and walked over to the guard.

"Sure. They say they gonna make smoking in jails illegal one of these days, ban cigarettes in places like this all across the nation," he said striking a match, cupping one hand and holding out the flame for her to light the smoke through the bars. Now, he whipped his wrist back and forth. Rolling whisps of grey smoke rose from the blackened stick in his hand.

"I'll believe it when I see it, Birch... thanks."

"No problem, you."

Now, she moved back to the bunk and rolled up a sleeve and held her arm out, studying the lines in her newest bird tattoo. It was a mocking bird. And she was clearing her throat and continuing her small jailhouse dissertation, saying,

"They're like clocks, man. They all need one thing, and once you figure out how to wind 'em up, just like a clock, they start ticking. They can't help it, and they don't know why, just like a clock can't help it. It doesn't know why it ticks. It just ticks."

"What's that?"

"What's what? What winds 'em up?"

"Yeah."

"Desire, Birch, desire. They all need... they all have to be desired. Don't mean desiring one'll get you one."

"How's that?"

"You gotta give it. Then, the most important thing you can do is take it from them and give it to someone else so they can see it. A woman won't be shown up by another woman like that."

"Hmm... and what about horses?"

"What about horses?"

"Like a horse? You said they're like horses. I am captivated. I have to hear this." Birch was leaning forward and smiling facetiously.

"You ever try to walk up to a horse?"

He shrugged.

"What happens?"

"I don't know."

"They walk away."

"So?"

"And what happens when you turn your back to them, and you walk away,

huh? I'll tell you what happens, they follow you, try to stick their heads in your business and get your attention. Try real hard, too. But the thing about a woman, Birch, is that they are a thousand times worse than any horse you've ever seen in your whole life."

"I never had a horse. Do I look like I know about horses? C'mon, lady."

"What about a woman? You ever had a woman? Look, what I'm saying's... a woman can't be showed up by another woman. I mean, of course, there are some. There always are exceptions, but by and large, my man, they won't have it. I've seen it a dozen times. Shoot, it's happening right now back in county. Girl comes in. Says she has a man, and she don't want women, anyway, and sure as hell don't want nothing to do with the shorthaired buck toothed women smiling at them when they get released into population with the rest of the girls.

So... it's like I say. They sneer at the attention when they get it, but a few days in, Birch, just a few days into it, the strangest thing happens, just like clockwork, Birch, just like a clock."

"Oh, yeah? What's that?"

"They learn that there's a system among the women or most of them. Enough of them, anyway."

"What system?" The guard pushed his bottom lip out and held his head back and squinted at the lanky girl with her orangish hair.

"You see, Birch, they learn that the ugly women smiling at them from the corners..."

"Like you?"

She smiled and nodded slowly at him, saying,

"Touché. Touché. Good one. Yeah. Like me. And what they find out is this. Their value, their place in the little jailhouse society, their position over the other women in the clutter is determined by ugly old me," and she wagged her head with every syllable as she said this, teasing and enjoying the naughtiness of what she was saying.

"Okay."

"Well, pull that attention, Birch. Give it to another girl right in front of them. Turn your back, and next thing you know is she's bringing you stuff and making your bed in the morning. Before night falls, shoot, sometimes before chow time, she's paying attention to you and begging you to make her yours. They fight for you, after that."

"Well, I done heard it all, now, girl! You just take it all, don't you?" He slapped his hands against his pants and laughed again, saying, "You a chauvinist. I never in my life..." He laughed harder.

"Is that supposed to be a bad thing?"

She pulled on her cigarette. The ember glowed orange, and she smiled, blowing smoke out into the cell and pushed her shoulder blades back into the brick wall behind her. There was a moment of silence, and the guard scratched his mustache and stared at the girl on her bunk through the bars and shook his head.

"What about you, girl?"

"What about me?"

"You ever loved someone?"

"I thought I did when I was young, once. My hillbilly woman, but I was a child, then, Birch, only a child. Got scarred real bad by it, almost killed me. And I learned that it was all a waste of time, Birch. Love is just a means of getting what I want."

"Don't you want it, though? I mean, you're a woman. Women love. They need love."

"Love? Love..." she asked and looked about the pitted concrete floor and replied flatly, now, "I don't know what love is Birch, and I don't think I'm capable of it. That's ok, though. That's how I want it."

For some time, the inmate stared up into the space above her head. She was studying the motes of dust swirling in the light. And it was silent. She didn't move or speak and looked sad. Then, she said,

"Women love, you said, huh? They need love, right? Isn't that right, what you said?"

"Yeah. They do. The ones I know."

"Maybe, they do. But maybe I ain't no woman, Birch."

"What are you a reptile?"

"Maybe... I mean... obviously not. But maybe."

"C'mon. You sure you ain't some kind of devil?"

"I just told you, Birch. I'm a witch, an enchantress. Maybe, I turn into a snake at night. I'll be a devil. That don't bother me. I'm the devil of Clatsop County this week. I'll be the devil somewhere else next."

And the two of them—the old guard named Birch and the girl who would spend the next several years in prison going by the nickname Bird—leaned forward for many minutes after that, smiling and almost laughing at the conversation.

THE GIRLS SLEPT TOGETHER in the daytime. Back on Eleonore's property, warmer days melted the still-cold nights. They spent their evenings wrapped up together in front of the fire or in Eleonore's bed.

Hair twirled between fingers.

Bird's black curls had grown longer and softer. And fingertips traced scars on one another's body. There were whispers of warm wet breath when they woke up together, words of love spoken into the sides of sweaty cheeks and foreheads, and the soft skin of Eleonore's ear pressed into Bird's—who was Samantha McCool—bony shoulder. They slept. They held each other.

The chores were done with laughter and hugging and smiles.

Some late mornings, Eleonore would bake a loaf of bread and pack a basket and take Bird on walks to eat under the green budding branches of a tree on the small hilltop across the property, and other times, she would start the tractor and show Bird how to change and use the attachments to make rows in the soil where she'd grown her garden every year.

This consummation of their hope, the communion of their flesh ushered in a paradise that was manifest between them. The property and the house had become a sort of temple. And they offered themselves—one to the other—on the altar of the mattress in

Eleonore's bedroom. It was bliss.

For Eleonore and for Bird, the world had previously been cold and hard. Now, it glowed. It had all become a secret garden. And one morning, Eleonore explained what Temple Garments[1] were and how she'd never taken hers off completely, even to bathe, before that first night with Bird.

"What do you mean?"

"Well, I bunch it up around my ankle or wrist or wherever and wash like that."

"Why?"

"We're not supposed to take them off."

"Ever?"

"Never. No one can enter into heaven without his garment," Eleonore looked at Bird and dragged a

____

[1] Temple Garments are given to Mormons in what is called an "endowment ceremony," as a sign of purity and devotion to God.

finger down her neck without thinking.

"Really?" Bird was staring. "But it's off, now. Why?"

Elenore shrugged and nodded with her head, slightly shrinking from her lover.

Bird pointed and looked down. An aged and wrinkled unitard sat crumpled on the floor. It was larger than anything Bird could wear, and she laughed. "Look how huge it is!" Bird pointed more emphatically and held her hand over her snicker.

Eleonore covered her own mouth and looked up at Bird.

"Come on. Let's go."

Eleonore followed Bird to the front of the house. It was where an old American flag hung from a pole on the house. It came down with some struggle from the women. Finally, Bird took the flag off of the rod and replaced it with the oversized undergarment.

The skinnier woman wore one of Beau's white tank tops that morning. It fit her like a short dress. And she stood with the hair of her armpits exposed in the sunlight, her big toe's opaque yellow disease on display. She laughed and saluted the undergarment mockingly and slapped Eleonore's stomach and hooted. Eleonore laughed meekly, and she didn't. She touched her lips and cowered with her posture, as if to hide her fat nakedness, and she tried to laugh, again, with her head down. She shuffled inside.

ELEONORE WOKE UP, one morning. Her ring finger was bare. It wasn't clear when it had happened. But it had come to pass, in some mysterious way, that the thin silver wedding band which she'd worn for all those years with Beau—when he was gone and when he'd been present—fit loosely on Bird's thumb. Eleonore grunted in the quiet. She burned with anger. And Bird was slumbering. She was slobbering on the pillow.

The serenity on her lover's face and the warmth of her body next to her disarmed Eleonore. Instead of worrying about the ring, she thought, now, of Beau. It was not long before he would return. And at first, Eleonore was panicked. But then, as time passed, she relaxed and imagined ways in which she might explain to him her predicament and how it had all happened and that she was not angry with him, that she held nothing against him for his failures as a husband. She wanted to tell him that, if she could and if there was a way, she would make it all go back and make their marriage work the way it was supposed to.

But there was not.

And it could not.

A new life had been given to her. A new creature existed where she once had. And there was no way in which this work could be undone or forgotten or hidden.

So, she went on embracing her new lover when she woke up. She was stuttering and gushing to her Birdy about nothing and noticing the ring on Bird's thumb and forgetting it and seeing it, again. They slept in the bed she had shared with Beau. They ate something around three in the afternoon. No fire was burning. The women got back into the warm bed together.

"Thank you, Birdy."

"For what?"

"For giving me this."

"Giving you what? You came to me, remember?"

Eleonore blushed and shook her head and pushed her nose into Bird's arm, saying,

"Heaven. Here with you, just like this... this is heaven for me, Birdy. That's what you gave me."

"Heaven? I don't think we're going to heaven," Bird laughed.

"No. Not like that, that's not what I mean. I mean..."

"Yeah? What do you mean?"

"I mean... well, that... You're everything I ever wanted. I prayed for you. I prayed for you to come to me for years, for my whole life, since I was a little girl... and here you are. Sometimes," Eleonore sniffed. She wiped her nose and spoke, "Sometimes, this is too much for me. I waited for you my whole life, and there's nothing, I think, can tear me away from you. There's nowhere I won't follow you and nothing I want that isn't you."

"Stop it."

"Stop?"

"C'mon," Bird said. "Don't do all this, right now. It's just too much. But you know..."

"Know what?" Eleonore was looking at the ring.

"Know that I love you."

The women smiled. They embraced and forgot where they were. They forgot what they were doing. It was warm and slow and quiet and there was a slight rain on the window behind their head.

NOW, SOMETHING STIRRED IN THE LIVING ROOM. Its shadow could be seen moving in the light beneath the door, a mad, black being come to execute judgment. Someone was there. Bird made a strange sound, a short and swallowing moan. It was involuntary, a reflex.

Eleonore was calm. She sat up and held the covers to her chest. The country woman was unhappy about the moment and all of it—regretting most of all that she and Bird were naked and that it would be in this state that Beau would find her. There was no real reason for her to expect what was coming. Beau had never been violent. And now, the bed was moving as if in an earthquake as Bird trembled and was paralyzed with panic.

The doorknob turned.

The large silhouette of the man stood in the doorway. There was the sound of an animal, but there was no animal. Eleonore's face paled.

Now, he stood by the bed. And the heavy, calloused hands landed blows on the women through the sheets. A sort of speechless choking came from the man's throat. He pulled the covers back. The soft, white bodies clutched themselves. They squirmed. They flailed and shrieked and bounced around the house as the broad man gave chase, landing blows on their backs and bodies with his fists and pulling their hair as they ran from him so that their skulls snapped back. They fell to the floor. They rose, again, and ran. And things were breaking.

Bird made it to the yard. Beau smashed the heavy glass candy dish over Eleonore's head. He stuck his fist into her stomach, so that she lay on the floor, breathless and teary-eyed. There was a moment of quiet.

He pursued Bird. He was bearing down on her. Eleonore watched it through the open door. And Bird fell down, her body steaming in the cold rain and sunlight and mud, stricken by fear.

For some moments, Bird knelt paralyzed and dumb. She was still. She was speechless like a toy or doll or idolatrous figurine—an unholy child trapped in her own nightmare—and Beau gripped the splitting maul. He dragged it, smilingly. It was slower than before. Everything was. The rage had settled, and now, his every movement was premeditated.

He would kill her, the way men had killed intruding animals in that part of the country for centuries. So, he held the maul over his head and drove it down at Bird. She held her wrist. She was protecting her face.

The heavy metal head of the tool bounced off of her elbow. And as he held it, once again, high above his head, ready to drop it on the cowering and frail Bird—this time, certain he would surely split the woman's skull or wound her so that her arm would dangle as if from a thread and blood would spurt across the yard—the rounder, shorter woman bounced on bare feet out of the house and through the mud.

Beau was slow, turning around.

He never saw Eleonore.

Now, the toll of a dull bell rang out in the yard. It was the peal of Eleonore's cast iron skillet on Beau's head. For a moment, he spun in the mud and stepped sideways. Eleonore took Bird's hand and led her to the house, still wielding the skillet. The man staggered up to the door. He stepped in and fell to his knees.

Eleonore swung, again. She was going for his face. There let out another peal from cooking pan.

Only this time, it was a mortal clang, and the man's body went limp like a wet rag falling to the floor. His arm stiffened violently, and his hand twisted unnaturally. Soon, fluid leaked from his nose and mouth. A round piece of bone covered his ear and hung by the tissue of his scalp. It had the appearance of a primitive mortar or crude and shallow dish for eating, and in the missing space—where his hair and scalp and skull were absent—the pink and wrinkled flesh of his brain was visible.

THE FAT WOMAN SAT ON THE FLOOR in a mound of her own soft white flab staring at the man she'd married so many years ago. Eleonore's fingers remained on the cast iron handle but were limp and pulsing. There were many moments of that, her staring, and it was silent except for the haunting, labored breath of the man before her. His eyes had glazed. She stared. He gurgled deeply. Bird moaned and rolled on the floor and sat with Elenore, both women sweating and breathing and bleeding in places.

"I'm going to get this off me," Bird stood and said after a long time. Mud on her skin had turned a lighter color and cracked so that she looked to be afflicted by a strange growth of scales or disease of the skin. "You okay?"

Silence was all Eleonore offered.

"Okay. I'll just be a minute." Bird said.

When she came back out into the living room, the door was still open.

Eleonore had not moved, even a little. And it was only after Bird had dressed in the same clothes in which she'd been found some six months prior—the thick leather jacket and tight denim and the red high-top shoes—and sat down next to Eleonore, again, that the fatter woman looked away from Beau. Her lip was quivering. The other woman's bad breath brought Eleonore out of her haze.

And she winced as she spoke, saying,

"Wish we could have talked one last time. I didn't think it would be like this."

"Don't be hard on yourself. He was going to kill me. You saved me."

Eleonore didn't speak.

The man coughed up a puddle of bloody phlegm and chunk and foam that hung from the side of his crooked mouth and stunk, and whatever breathing he did could not be seen.

There was no rise. There was no fall of his chest, but a small irregular wheeze came from deep within the blackness of his open mouth. A paradise had sprung forth in the women's time alone together there on the farm, but now it lay fallen and desolate in the body of the man who—more and more, moment by moment—was grey and wearing the stillness of death.

"They'll give us the chair for this Eleonore." Bird paced and tapped her fingertips together and leaned forward and whispered, "We have to get out of here, E. We have to go."

"I know," the woman said, still naked and on the floor—a spatter of Beau's blood had dried on her chin, and there was blood on her ear that had run from a cut in her scalp.

"Let's see... let's see... Do you have any money or jewelry?"

Elenore stood.

Her hair—which she'd taken to keeping uncovered in Bird's presence but twisted so she would not trip—had come undone and tripped her. She took a moment and bound it around her skull and let whatever length remained hang over her shoulder. There was a drawer of tools and batteries and flashlights and the like in the kitchen, and she walked to it and returned to the living room and pushed the coffee table and lifted the rug from underneath it.

The hammer's claw slid under a floorboard and bit into the wood. Eleonore pulled the handle. A sharp tooth pressed into her bottom lip. And the nails came out of the joists in an ellipsis of one, two, three strange and high-pitched honks. Her arm disappeared into the blackness underneath and reappeared with a mud caked mason jar. Its contents made muted noise as she walked into the bedroom and returned with two small leather pouches and a satchel.

"What's that?" Bird asked, putting a knee on the armrest of the couch.

But Eleonore didn't speak. She unscrewed the lid of the jar and poured out its contents. Then, she pulled out what was in the pouches. After that, she opened the satchel and held it forward for Bird to see. There was a dozen or so gold coins inside of it. On the table lay many stacks of American bills.

"How much is it?"

Eleonore shrugged, indifferent, and put it all back and said,

"We can take the truck. There's a store of fuel in the barn for the tractor that we can bring with us. I'm going to get cleaned up and dressed and pack some things."

"How long till someone finds out, E? Huh? How long will it be till someone comes out here and finds him?"

Eleonore shook her head and looked at Beau, now completely still and silent, and almost blubbered but stopped it and said,

"I don't know. It's hard to say."

"Does anyone come out here for anything?"

"Get the tank filled every August. Sometimes, I sell a cow. Of course, there's the bank and that, but I never seem them, not hardly."

Eleonore said this while picking a piece of the shattered candy dish from the blubber of her leg, and now, she pinched the small shard and held it close to her face as if it were a germ or flea which had been living on her—it was bloodless—and she tossed it on the floor.

She was naked and fat. She was very white, standing there, and the sun was shining in through the window so that she seemed to emit some kind of pale aura the way an angel or apparition might, themselves, glow or radiate some other worldly light, and she touched the amulet around her neck and tilted her head as she turned down the hall.

"What about his work?" Bird asked.

"I don't know."

"You don't know?" Bird was, now, looking at the pink in the creases of Eleonore's many folds of fat in her back.

Eleonore shook her head and looked down and steadied herself against the wall. And she said in a low and deflated tone,

"I'm getting cleaned up, and we'll get everything and go. I just wish we could have talked. It would have been so much nicer. I never meant for it to be like this, Bird. I never meant it." Again, her face twisted in despair, but she took a step and stopped. She took another and stopped, and finally, turned into the bathroom.

BY AFTERNOON, they lugged a chest of clothes and some blankets into the back of the truck. The girls carried on their backs the five cannisters of gasoline from the barn grunting through the house and out into the driveway and dropped them in squeaking thumps next to the chest and other things they'd packed into it. Birds were chirping. A soft wind knocked in the tree branches on the far side of the garden.

The girls looked like refugees. They were fugitives—derelict and banished from their estate. Eleonore walked back and grabbed the.22 rifle out of the closet and went out to the barn and patted her cows on their heads. She grimaced and touched the barrel of the .22 to one of the animals' heads. But she could not. And she let the chickens out of their coop and walked back to the truck. With watery eyes, Eleonore tossed the key to Bird.

That old engine turned in its low humming rhythm. And the tires rolled through the mud and grass between the two trees—Eleonore's trees— that pair of formidable Chinkapin Oaks showing their new growth and which had grown tremendously since the first time Eleonore had seen them and which are still there, today. She was sad to pass them, to see them go. They were her friends.

The girls bounced in the truck. Their movement was slow. Bird gripped the wheel tightly. And it was right about where the gravel did kick up against the truck doors on the easement road—and does to this day—that Eleonore asked,

"Where are we going?"

Bird looked forward and bit her lips from the inside and cocked her head. Now, she stuck her tongue out and said,

"Got some stuff. Some

people to see about off the coast."

Bird shifted. The engine hummed. Eleonore spoke again,

"I just wish I could have talked to him. There's things I'd like to have said. There are things he needed to know."

"He's dead, Eleonore. He's dead. Everyone's nicer when they're dead. Always is. He was going to kill me. Now, you have me."

Darkness was settling over the land, there. And Eleonore didn't speak. She stared forward. There was a handful of stars visible when they came off of the woods. They pulled onto the highway. And Bird pushed the accelerator heading west.

BIRD AND ELEONORE DROVE ALL NIGHT. They stopped on the side of the black highway outside of Jerome to empty a few of the gas cans they'd brought with them. There they stood and saw the lights of the town. In the moments that followed, dry grass cracked under their feet as they stepped out into an open field and squatted silently under the stars. It was only once they crawled back into the truck and were driving that either one spoke since they left the old brick house on the remote mountain farm.

"What were you doing there that night?"

"What night?"

"That night we found you?" Elenore pinched one hand in the fingers of the other.

"Ahh..." Bird was steady as she spoke. There was an unsettling disinterest in her voice. It was even and cold and said, "You found me in a rest stop, right?"

"A small washhouse on the side of the highway outside of Pocatello, close to the house."

"I know."

The small crackle of Eleonore licking her dry lips could be heard in the cab of the truck. The fatter woman leaned forward and rubbed an elbow.

"I was... Well, I was in prison for almost seven years."[1]

"You never told me that."

"I didn't want to. You didn't ask, either."

"Well, why would I?"

"You wouldn't..." there was a pause, and Bird downshifted as the highway upon which they rode wound through a small town called Wendell. "You wouldn't have asked.

And I wouldn't have told you or wanted to tell you, well, because it's painful. All of it is painful..."

"What is?"

"Prison."

"And?"

"And why you found me how you found me."

As Bird spoke more and more in the heated cab of the truck, her breath began to stink worse than it had ever had at the house with Eleonore. It was combination of the cramped space and heat and the anxiety of being stuck. And Eleonore looked out of her window. She swiveled her head as they passed a boot on the side of the road. Now, she asked,

"And why'd we find you like that?" The woman could feel herself suspended over the world in a surreal way, using the banter to ignore the dreadful weight of the murder she'd committed against her own husband.

---

[1] Keeping track of Bird's history is difficult. Of course, there are all the usual reasons for our uncertainty concerning her life, such as people's misunderstandings, embellishments, and the like. Yet, with her, the lack of clarity surrounding her life and history is only exacerbated by her own lies and apparent inability to be honest to those with whom she was closest.

She was angry. She was sad. She was thrashing inside of herself to make it stop, to make it go away. Bird's breath was appalling. But for now, Eleonore focused on her questions and the words Bird spoke in response.

"I had a wife in there, in prison, you know."

"I don't know anything about that." Eleonore said flatly. She was tense and clenching her teeth and thought for a second and softened.

Bird paused. She checked in the dark for some clue in Eleonore's face or breathing or movement but found none and spoke, hesitantly, again.

"Her name was Lavonne. She had a brother who we called the Joker, and while I was in there, she wrote him, and he wrote her, and there were plans made for us to rob a bank. You see, Lavonne was in there before me on a robbery, and she was getting out a little more than a year after me. So, me and Joker, we were going to get things ready. When Lavonne got out, we'd do it."

There was a long silence. Some droplets of rain hit the windshield. The road rose steadily and slowly. The highway ended, and Bird turned right and muttered something about needing to get a road map soon. Eleonore sat with her arms crossed, now, and said,

"Then, what?"

"Then, what? Well, Lavonne never got out. They heard from another girl in there that she'd confessed to killing a man and his wife in cold blood long before her robbery. It was a famous case in Florida..." Bird stopped for a moment, remembering the woman named Lavonne and that time of her life and continued, "And so when she should have gotten out, they shipped her to Florida instead. Far as I understood, she was guilty and convicted before she got off the bus."

The headlights of a truck passed them. And for a second, their faces and bodies formed themselves out of the blackness—obscure and formless blobs momentarily ascending into a higher order—and in an instant, they disintegrated back into their featureless existences in the dark. For some time, the world was only what the truck's headlights touched, the worn black road and the dry grass and trees floating by them. A pair of small red taillights were visible and were not and were, again, as they drove the bending highway. Eleonore pulled at her collar. She cracked the window and held her mouth to it, escaping the stench of the other woman.

"So…"

"Me and Joker, we had it all planned out for months by that point. We were up in Olympia. And we didn't want to lose what we had, so we recruited one of his buddies. We did it, and I had the escape planned out perfectly. Last thing was for us to switch cars down in Salt Lake City," and at this, Bird laughed smally and bitterly to herself. "Yup," she said, "We got to Salt Lake. Changed out vehicles and were on our way up to Spokane. That's where they were going to drop me off with my share of the loot."

"What happened."

"You found me, didn't you? Joker and his buddy—a guy named Darius or so he said—beat the living hell out of me, Eleonore."

For a moment, Eleonore's repugnance for the woman gave way to worry and compassion for the injustice which the more fragile Bird had suffered, as she listened to the story. It was only for a moment. Eleonore remembered the ring and how Bird had taken it, and now, she wondered if the name she'd given was her name at all and if this strange, lanky lesbian had merely used her and her home as a place for hiding out.

Eleonore asked,

"Is that why you had a wig?"

"Wig?"

"Yes. A blonde wig. I found it at the washhouse."

"Oh, yeah. I forgot."

"And what is your name?"

"My name?"

"It isn't Bernadette, is it?"

"Samantha. My name is Samantha."

"Samantha what?"

"McCool. Sam McCool."

"What about..." Eleonore stopped. She didn't want to know about the ring or why the woman had taken it and worn it. Talking wasn't working. And the fat woman blubbered, pushing her palm into her teeth and choked in dramatic sobs. Her body quivered. The back of her wrist passed across her nose. Eleonore pushed the palm of her hand into the cold window and dragged it across the glass.

They came over a hill and saw the lights of Boise and stopped at a 24-hour grocery store. Bird got out. She returned to the truck with cigarettes and some food and held a few small bills and the coinage from the change out to Eleonore who took it and wiped her nose and mouth and studied the contents of the bag. There were pork rinds in a bag and two Coca-Colas and a few sandwiches.

In the other bag, there was a six-pack of Pabst Blue Ribbon sweating in the plastic. Bird reached into it and grabbed one and popped it open. Her throat glugged down half the can or more, and the woman lit a cigarette. It was late. It was chilly, and the wind blew.

"Well, I think we'll find a place to rest up till morning light."

"Okay." Pink splotches showed on Eleonore's face in the parking lot light. She sniffled.

Now, they parked behind a church. The truck sat next to a dumpster. It was hidden among some small pine trees. In the light from the parking lot next door, the skinnier woman dawdled in the dirt. Her feet moved randomly through the tall grass around the truck. And she leaned in. She pressed herself against Eleonore and turned on the radio and scanned the dial and danced to music. It was the first the radio had been played.

Eleonore ate her sandwich and another and then some of the pork skins. She drank a coke. That was all followed by a burp, and she asked,

"What about the ring?" Eleonore called out through the open window.

"What about it?" The words came out in a cloud of cigarette smoke.

"Why'd you take it?"

The black-haired lesbian pulled for a long time on her cigarette and leaned back dramatically. The ember glowed orange. There was something different about her after a few beers.

She said,

"I'm your husband."

"You're my husband?" Eleonore sniffed.

"You're my wife. My country bumpkin wife who loves to eat," Bird wagged her head and showed her teeth in sarcastic cruelty.

"But you're not a man. You're not my husband."

"Oh, yeah? Well, what about..." she walked over to Eleonore's open window and blew cigarette smoke and breathed on her and slapped the woman across the ear and jaw and kissed her. It was quiet. And the taller woman stood there in the light from the street lamp over the trees. Bird was stiff and smirking strangely as if revealing in herself, in that moment, something else, something new and dangerous and scary.

Eleonore's whole body tensed.

Bird smoked and said,

"Look, this is what it is. I get it... you're scared. It's a bad situation, but it's not my first rodeo, and you're not my first married woman, so come off it," and she pulled Eleonore's hair a moment so that the fatter woman yipped in pain. "Move over. I'm getting in."

THE SKY TURNED PINK WITH MORNING. Bird turned the key. Eleonore woke up and stretched and looked over at her driver drinking the last half of a flat beer. It was quiet. No one was out. There were no cars on the road, and they moved easily across the dry rock landscape.

The sun ascended behind them. It followed them as they drove, and

In Portland, Bird demanded money from Eleonore and used it to stay for an unknown number of days in a drab motel called The Joyce. It was downtown. Their room was on the third floor. The first night Bird bought scissors and a box of black hair dye and some clippers along with some tape and beer and other items. She put Eleonore in a chair and cut almost four feet of that long hair and pushed the fatter woman's head into the sink to dye it. Then, she stood in front of the mirror herself and shaved the sides of her head so that she looked like a boy and washed and put on a knit cap. She taped her chest. She was pretending to be a man.

With nothing holding her back, Bird was drinking liquor and staggering and slurring her words. And the patinaed and worn band—which had been given to Eleonore by Beau all those years before and which was now on Bird's knobby thumb—came up, again. Subtle agitation worked in the bodies of the women. Slight animation turned into jaws thrust forward and a pointing finger and the thud of a closed fist on the dresser. Voices slowly rose. Now, there were screams and flailing limbs.

Bird repeated that she was Eleonore's husband. Eleonore told her that she was no man, at all, and not a husband. She could not be. And in return, Bird did gross exaggerations of the farm woman's modesty and puffed out her cheeks like she was fat and said plainly that Eleonore had never pleased her the way a woman could and, indeed, never would. Eleonore hurled some insult back. She didn't know what she said. But it was the first time that she could remember having ever screamed or raising

her voice, at all, in anger toward anyone. The loose brass of light fixtures on the wall vibrated as Eleonore stomped her foot on the floor.

And like a poison, she drank it in and screamed and was sitting on the bed and standing, again, to stomp and put her finger in Bird's face and was pushed to the ground and dragged by her hair to the window and stood up—so that she felt the cool night mist on her face and where her shirt had opened and saw the traffic and a trolley car rattling on its tracks. Bird pushed her from behind as if out of the window and pulled her by the hair, again. The slender boy-like figure pushed its palm into the stubbier woman's face and into the wall and choked her. The grit of a dry and putrid-smelling, tastebud tongue licked Eleonore's eyelid.

"I'm your husband. You're my wife." The stench emanating from whatever scales of plaque clung to the back of Bird's throat pushed, warm and stomach-turning, into Eleonore's face, a rancid metabolized liquor. Tall legs straddled the shorter, fatter hips. Nose touched cheek. One body obscenely pressed into the other, and a hand ripped some fabric and slid under Eleonore's shirt and moved violently. "Okay?"

"Okay." Eleonore was sniffling and shaking. Her face was hot.

"Don't you love me?"

Eleonore nodded.

"You love me, right?"

"Yes."

"Say it!" Bird's teeth were clenched. Bird's words were slurring and hands jerked.

"I love you."

"You want to live without me?"

Eleonore shook her head.

"Are you sure? I can leave. We can end this, tonight, and I can go find someone else, someone who loves me."

"I love you." Eleonore was choking and blubbering, and her mouth was snotty. A bubble started and expanded. It popped.

"Okay, then," Bird said releasing the grip on Eleonore's throat and pushed her away, "Now, go get in bed and get ready for your husband."

THE CLANG AND CLAP OF A GARBAGE TRUCK and a voice screaming through the empty street below woke Eleonore. She was rubbing her face in the half dark. And down the hall, outside of the communal bathroom and shower, she met a dwarfish man with wrinkled, yellow skin in a towel. His body was covered in black spots like smears of ink—old tattoos which had faded. And she nodded to him and washed herself and walked back to the room and sat up in bed.

Eleonore was staring at Bird's face. It was swollen with sleep. It was smushed between the pillows, and the mouth hung open, breathing loudly and slowly. For a long time, the woman sat there in the sunlight studying the motes swirling in the room and wondered about how things had escalated so quickly. She touched her neck, where it hurt and where she thought she might be bruised.

Thoughts of Beau and how he'd labored to breathe on the floor and turned grey and stopped breathing altogether came to her. There was fear. There was sadness. It was strange to be banished from the farm and to know that she had killed her very own husband in a moment of passion—a moment of panic to save the woman with whom she now shared a bed—and it was terrifying to be a fugitive hiding in that grimy motel from the cold, wet world outside. Eleonore choked for a moment. Images of Beau turning cold came to her. She shut her eyes, shaking her head.

And now, the warm body—in whom she placed all of her hope and which treated her with such cruelty—moved and stretched under the covers next to her. Skin brushed skin. Bird's fingers walked playfully up Eleonore's leg and arm and pinched her face. They laughed. There were pecks on the forehead and yawns and a long hug. This was it. There was nowhere else to go and nuzzling the warm skin of her lover was the only way to keep the fantasy they'd created from being lost forever. It hadn't hurt so badly.

"You ready to get up?"

"Yeah. You?"

"I'm up."

They laughed, and Eleonore asked,

"What are we doing?"

"Got to get some clothes. Got to get ready to get out of town. Sell the truck."

"Sell the truck, huh?"

"Yeah. And get out of here, once we do."

"And where are we going, again?"

"Olympia."

So, they stood and stretched and dressed and put together a pocketful of money to spend. And it was at a store on Burnside that Bird pointed to various records of psychedelic music and spoke with the excitement of a child. They drank tea from paper cups in a park on Glisan. And in a secondhand store in the Pearl District, Eleonore came out of a dressing room struggling with a belt and a pair of jeans.

"I'm having trouble getting these on."

"Let me see." Bird said.

"Look."

"I'm looking."

"Well, I can't get this belt on. It's too small." She was exasperated. Eleonore looked in the mirror as Bird knelt to help her fasten the jeans and said, "I don't know. I think these make me look fat."

"That's because you are fat." Bird said, yanking the belt.

"Ow."

"Ow, what?"

"That hurt."

"What do you want me to do, huh?"

Eleonore bit her hand. She hid in the dressing room for some minutes, while Bird spoke softly to her, apologizing. Soon, it was forgotten. And by sunset, they sold the truck to a man in a Safeway parking lot just over the river in Washington.

THEY PULLED INTO OLYMPIA THAT NIGHT, bouncing in the front seat of a loud Buick that was the color of a kidney bean except for the places where it had been dented and paint flaked from the body. Bird lit a cigarette and opened a beer. Thick white foam fizzed from the can and dripped on the ground under the streetlamp. The woman licked it. It was warm outside. And the black world around them buzzed with insects.

Bird used a key[1] to get into a gate and then into a storage unit and grunted as she lugged several boxes and a black, leather trunk into the Buick and some other things and placed them into the backseat. There was an old boarding house. It had been standing in the hills outside of Washington's capitol city for most of a century. Prospectors and loggers lived there, once, a haggard population of migratory workers in dirty long johns and suspenders. And the current residents of that same building were just as dirty and just as haggard, only their wages were earned dishonestly. Some were the recipients of welfare checks. A number had come home from the war and were lost or maimed or both. And all were waiting. They were waiting and wasting away and standing around, forever waiting for something or someone or nothing at all.

An old sign out front said the words,

"Welcome to Hotel St. Vincent."

The wide and wooden, two-level building had a courtyard and long exterior porches which were covered. Dead bugs and leaves and cigarette butts littered the grass. The room the girls rented had a small kitchenette. By the window was a place where the tiles had been ripped off the floor and clumps of old mastic remained. There was a leaning bed with a lumpy mattress. There was rust on an obsolete and disconnected radiator by the window, and there were freckles of a green

---

[1] One of the two keys which had been on the amulet around Eleonore's neck.

mold on the walls and ceiling by the toilet. It smelled like old sweat and dust and cobweb.

THEY CARRIED THEIR THINGS UP INTO THE ROOM and unpacked. Bird carried up a bag of rice. Then, she set out a small, buckled baby's shoe made of leather and filled it with rice and placed it in the window and sat beholding it for some time moving her mouth slowly and silently as if remembering an argument or whispering an old incantation. And she dug through a box of files on the bed. Bird opened a beer and took a drink.

"See," she threw a folder onto the bed where Eleonore lay, "This is the paperwork...social security cards, birth certificates, pieces of mail, uh...." Bird picked a piece of something from between her teeth and studied it and put it on her tongue, "uh... what else do we have here? Oh yeah, we got heat bills and files of whatever else we need."

"Where did you get them?"

"Collected them while we were waiting on the bank job. There's a girl I'm going to contact in the next few days to see if she can get us more. It'll only last us so long before the information won't work."

"This one is a man's...Tom Sayers. Who's that..."

"For me." The boyish figure was hunched over a pair of gangly, cupped hands, lighting a cigarette and snatched the papers from Eleonore.

They drove down into Oregon and systematically hit the small towns up to Tacoma and east of Seattle. At each stop, they used wigs which Bird had brought and makeup and stuffed cotton balls into their cheeks to alter their likenesses. Now, they had new names. Several of Eleonore's ID cards labeled her a Mrs. Aftersen, they wore their disguises and deposited small amounts of Eleonore's cash into bank accounts to get American Express credit cards. It took days. And at night, they drove back to the old flophouse where they slept.

BIRD DRANK. Mostly it was beer. On such afternoons and evenings, the haranguing was minimal, but when there was a bottle of liquor sloshing around the room or upturned and glugging in the bed until it was empty, then it was terrible.

Bird stumbled and slurred—breathing her putrid breath on her fat companion and blew cigarette smoke. Elenore's hair was pulled. The orange glowing ember of a cigarette popped and sizzled, as Bird held her down and extinguished it in the fat of Eleonore's skin. Then, Bird pushed the mouth of the bottle to thicker woman's lips. Then, Eleonore drank and was drunk. Then, she was stupid.

Eleonore's face drooped with the alcohol. Her lips thinned and turned up in a strange menacing crimp. She was bleeding from her mouth—blood smeared on her teeth—and did hold the bottle herself. She was the one who drank from it, now. And they fought. And some nights, Bird pushed her palm into Eleonore's face or flung lit cigarettes at her and threw things around the room or threatened to leave and did and was gone for hours—or a whole night— before coming back.

The deflated Eleonore stumbled in the fine brown dust of the parking lot on those nights. When the Buick was gone, Eleonore clenched her fists. She bit her lip. She screamed until strands of slobber hung from her chin and spun around in the dirt. Then, she would go back up to the room. There the woman would wait and speak softly out into the room, as if Bird was there, and say she was sorry and that she knew she was wrong and would do anything to have her back. Eleonore curled up and cried on the mattress.

BUT IN THE MORNINGS, they made up. The two reconciled with heavy breaths. There were tearless yammering words of contrition and admission and hugs after that.

Eleonore pressed her ear to Bird's clavicle and held her hand out and hugged her lover around the room, and Bird traced the lines in the fatter woman's face and forehead and read from a book about Virgos and what the current astrological bodies meant for them—that it was a time of great metamorphosis, a great change was coming and was, already, underway. After those sessions, the mannish lesbian would stand and lean over and kiss her redneck woman's forehead or trace the creases in Eleonore's palms with the dark tips of her own fingers over the bedsheets, the moving fingers of their interlocked hands like children's. It was bliss, again. It was peace for the moment.

Eleonore had nightmares and did her best to keep the crumbling dwelling as clean as she could. As the mornings drew on, she reached over and drank from the can or bottle in Bird's hand. It was as the stars said. Eleonore was no longer who she'd been. She was no longer the quiet and pious, country woman.

Although, some of the lonely Mormon wife's appearance and manners remained, the long colorless hair had disappeared. What still hung from her scalp was black and badly dyed. When she looked in the mirror she was shrinking. Her skin sagged and hung from her bones. Dramatic jowls jiggled along her jaw, and she had sunglasses on and lipstick and bruises on her neck and was a practitioner of that which was unnatural, by her own volition, and she smiled when she thought of it. She wore thinner dresses without leggings, now. She was smoking cigarettes. She cursed.

The frypan murder of the harelipped man she'd married as a teenager and the lesbian love affair which had preceded that crime had given her a new life.

Eleonore licked her teeth. She flipped through the fake ID cards and whispered the names to herself as she read them. A pair of her own fat fingers touched her lips when she thought of herself as another woman's property—a thought of her own invention. It was violent. It was dangerous. She was swooning silently to herself and held her breath.

In the afternoons, while Bird slept off the buzz of her beers, Eleonore wore little to cover herself on the bed and let clouds of blue cigarette smoke out of her mouth and watched them rise to the brown ceiling tiles. The strange bauble strung around her neck moved in her hand. She lay back on the bed, holding the charm, and breathed in this new world with its peculiar taste and its smell, the intoxicating atmosphere, and as one who is tired and resigned, drew the veil of a strange sleep over herself.

She was awake and smoking her cigarette.

Only now, life was a dream—a dream whose dreamer was, perhaps, a beast or animal or some other such base creature left wounded and made irrational, the way young mothers bereft of their children grieve and rage without thought, the way monsters hate and seek to destroy their makers.

Eleonore pushed the ember of her cigarette into the ashtray.

She twisted it into a powdery mess of

smoldering ash and extinguished crumbs.

She stood, now, and looked through the window. It was pink and red outside, as if the evening sky was dripping through the trees. She thought of the world and all that waited for her and the lonely, scared thing she had been for all those years lying dead somewhere within it. The woman lit another cigarette. She looked back towards the mattress, a breathing pair of limp and hairy legs, the swollen face hidden in the sheets.

Eleonore was ready.

She was tired of waiting.

THEY LEFT IN THE MORNING. The first pair of weeks on the road passed in a moment. It was exhilarating.

More than a hundred jewelry stores could be located in cities like San Francisco and Los Angeles and Seattle. And that number doubled when the surrounding communities were included. Portland had less. But it had enough. And so, the pair put on whatever disguise they used to get whichever ID and credit card they were had in their hands at the moment. And they went into the stores.

First, they bought wardrobes of high-end clothing and purses and leather wallets which they kept stuffed full of small bills wrapped in the larger denominations and walked into the jewelry stores—a dozen or more each day—and made purchases for expensive watches and diamond studded bracelets. They wore all of it.

They presented themselves as rich. And as Eleonore handled a tiara, Bird prodded with a finger in her back and urgent whispers in her ear. The owner straightened his back. He offered sideways, suspicious glances at the frail and oddly tall husband of the couple. He placed the item back in the case and hesitated. A bead of sweat showed on his nose. So, Bird unlatched the purse on Eleonore's shoulder and grabbed a wad of cash offering to,

"Pay in cash... we can always pay in cash. It's just so much more convenient on the card. In fact, dear," she said to Eleonore in her horn-rimmed glasses, "We can find something somewhere else...let's."

The man blushed. He replied,

"No, um, now you know... I don't think... I don't think that's necessary. We'd love to keep the business. No sense in making it harder than it needs to be for you," and laughed softly and put the item in a box and bowed as his worker slid the credit card in their machine.

AND ELEONORE WAS SMOKING. And she wore her disguises for days at a time. And she became these other women with their personalities and fragmented. Eleonore was driving and drove through the night while Bird slept, and she smoked. She was always smoking.

Each false identity, according to Bird's whispered words, could be used for a couple days before it was compromised and must be abandoned. It was laborious. There was no rest and only one stay in a bed at a hotel in that first fortnight on the road. They washed in gas station bathrooms. And they paid for all of it with the money Eleonore took from the house.

They got back to the room in Olympia on a Thursday afternoon and spent one night. There were two distinct fights that night, one in which the small mirror in the corner was cracked and Eleonore's head bled and a second spat during which Eleonore puked up white, opaque sludge through the window into the rain and knocked Bird's baby shoe full of rice into a black puddle below causing the fight to stop and Bird to fret.

In the morning, the shoe was replaced in the windowsill and filled with rice. Plane tickets to Philadelphia were purchased with cash at a travel agency in Tacoma. And they flew out of Seattle that night.

On the east coast, they rented a car and used the same—soon to be useless—identities to sell their jewelry to small jewelers outside of Philadelphia and Atlantic City and Trenton and just one larger outlet in the suburbs of Dover. Then, they spent two nights resting in a hotel with a casino in the lobby. It was on the boardwalk in Atlantic City. They took pictures in photobooths. Eleonore won a large stuffed frog at one of the tents with carnival games. Bird gambled at the blackjack tables and lost

and pulled her hair and bought more chips and lost and bought more and walked away with nothing. It was a brief vacation. And they never rested. There was a roving in Bird's eyes which Eleonore could not ignore. And they fought.

They slept till late afternoon, until the heat sweltered and they were sticky with sweat and could no longer stay in bed. And they drank through straws from tall glasses with umbrellas and fruit, so that the lines in their faces softened in the sun, and they smiled stupidly and screamed and stumbled under a boardwalk and kissed. Sand was in their hair. Sand was in their mouths. It was everywhere, and before they got back to the hotel, an argument started. At midnight, the hotel manager and one of his bellhops knocked on their door. He asked them if everything was alright and,

"Would you ladies, please, watch the noise? We've had complaints. Unfortunately, it is our policy to call the police if such things persist."

A drunk bird stared at his lapel and said,

"No problem. She's just giving me a hard time. You understand, right?" so unintelligibly that the manager squinted at her and nodded politely and left without a word. The door shut.

The next morning, they landed in Seattle and drove back to the flophouse and readied themselves for another spree down the west coast. This time, they used new identities for another two busy weeks. They visited the same towns but none of the same stores. And it was the same as before. Only this time, techniques for building confidence in the salesmen and storeowners had been honed. Eleonore took charge and prodded Bird to go for the more expensive, riskier items. And they recuperated in the splintery old room in Olympia for a night and bought tickets to Atlantic City, again, and flew back to Olympia and did it all, one more time. On the final trip east, they flew to Miami.

And when they got back to that damp and trashy room in Washington state—after more than eight weeks of being on the road and flying back and forth to the east—the two collapsed into bed and did not leave the room for several days. A newly purchased box fan was humming in the window. There was an open piece of luggage resting in the middle of the room while they slept. A mess of cash filled it, poured out onto the floor. And among the dollar bills were shining accessories like watches and bracelets and rings.

One of the girls coughed in the bed. A toenail scratched a leg and kicked off the sheets that smelled like sweat and old beer.

Now, the slow rhythmic breathing of exhausted sleep began, again. The women were worn out and hugging in the sheets and slobbering on their pillows and on each other.

They were snoring. It was late August. And as the day turned to night, mosquitoes—somehow snuck into their room through the window screens—did bite them and caused them to slap their bodies, until one got up to shut the window, and they were sleeping, again. They were so tired. It had only been two months. But they'd been to many places and done many things and slept so little and were haggard. Now, they were home with nothing left to do for a long time. Now, they were sleeping.

THE DAYS STRETCHED INTO WORDLESS and miserably hot voids of nothing to do and no one to see and nothing to feel. It was as if life and the world stopped for Eleonore. Only the sad figures inhabiting the rooms around them were still slowly milling around outside. The mixture of extreme boredom over time and the inevitable, growing pile of empty bottles and beer cans around the bed led to fighting and fussing. But now, something was happening. A stranger was coming around.

The small blonde-haired girl first showed up with Bird on the last Tuesday morning in August that year. It was after Bird left Eleonore in the middle of a spat. And when the girl—introduced as Crystal—came into the room with Bird, Eleonore did not see her. So, she stood up from the bed and was mostly naked and walking toward her lover for a hug and saying she was sorry and that she wouldn't do it—whatever it was—again.

But when she saw this new and other, smaller female, a female obviously invited into the room by and friendly with Bird, Eleonore's shriveled, naked body stopped mid step, as if silently and mortally wounded by a quick arrow through the heart or lungs. She stood rigid. She staggered as one whose organs are hemorrhaging. Eleonore's eyes turned up to Bird. Her face was supplicant.

"She's gonna get our new batch of papers." Bird said. "You got a cigarette?"

Eleonore fingered one out of the soft paper pack of Winstons in her lap. She pinched and handed it over. And Bird handed that cigarette back to the wiry frame of the young girl behind her who took it and looked down and folded her arms, and after some moments of awkward expectant staring from Bird, Eleonore handed over another. Bird struck a match and lit the three cigarettes and waved out the match. And the three of them stood there smoking with no words.

Bird was looking at the girl with blonde hair and dirty feet who was looking down. And Eleonore found it hard to stand or breathe. She was shaking. Her mouth hung open. And Eleonore sat on the bed for some time shaking her head, as if denying the reality which she beheld or looking for something which she had not yet seen.

And for some time, the girl stood by the door just as she'd come in with her arms folded and shivering. Only she was smoking. Her clothes looked to be wet and dirty. There were crumbs of leaves and grass in her hair like she slept outside. She wore sandals. And as the time went on, Bird took the girl by the hand. She sat her in the old wooden chair, so that both she and Bird faced away from Eleonore. And they spoke.

This new girl listened. Bird talked with familiarity. But it was hard to hear what they said, because the fan was running. And Eleonore sat back against the headboard of the bed in disbelief and smoked and was watching with a curled lip, thinking to herself that the girl looked atrophied and pathetic and sounded just as weak and stupid as she looked, and Eleonore was shaking her head and wondering to herself and how she'd come to think such terrible things about another person and was, again, scornful of and even disgusted by the sight of the girl whose hair Bird now petted and whose face Bird now touched and whose cigarette Bird pinched and put to her own lips.

Bird was leaning forward, over the girl, and asked questions. And there were answers. The girl spoke with a shamed face and in a hushed voice. And Eleonore was deeply troubled by all of it and thought to speak—to pretend that she was not affected—but was struck dumb and could not and

was fumbling with a pair of stockings and wiping her forehead and standing at the window, smoking and biting her nails and shifting her weight from bare foot to bare foot. And she was watching Bird. She was watching the pair talk.

Now, stars did begin to show themselves in the sky overhead through the pastel dust of clouds. And now, the air was still, and the skin of all three—the half-staggering Eleonore, the frowning blonde folding her arms with the torn belly shirt and the hyper-focused Bird—did shine with perspiration and grease, and Bird said,

"We're going to go, now," to Eleonore.

"Hmm...? Ugh. Um." Eleonore was struggling to make a coherent sound, to say a word with meaning. Her heart was beating. And her legs were weak. "Okay, where?" finally came out of her mouth.

"Get her a burger or something. She's hungry."

"Hungry?"

"Yeah."

"Okay."

"Besides, she needs me to take her somewhere for us."

"For us?"

"Yeah. For us."

Eleonore was looking at Bird's feet and looked up and saw the girl behind her and looked down, again. She scratched the back of her neck. There was nothing she could say, nothing she could think to say. And she sat down on the bed and reached over and flipped the switch on the fan. Now, feet moved and Bird looked in the mirror. The keys jingled in her hand, and she said,

"Let's go, you ready?" to the girl who nodded and shrugged at Eleonore with wide eyes, embarrassed and confused.

THE DOOR SHUT, and Eleonore sat there for some time. She was staring and wringing her hands. Everything that had just happened right in front of her left her wounded her and left her reticent about what to do or if what she had seen was real or not. It was real. She knew it was real but struggled to believe it. And after those moments alone in the slowly darkening room, she put on a thin, short gown over her underwear and walked down the stairs.

Eleonore saw Bird holding the blonde girl's hand and whispering in her ear. They were pushed up against the car. They were kissing.

Like a dream, Eleonore was yelling and standing behind the car and saw the red lights and was bumped to the ground. And now, she stood in a cloud of dust glowing in the headlights of the Buick and had her hands up and was screaming and, now, was rolling off of the hood of the car and spinning and thudding on the ground as she landed on her hip. She was hurt and was not and was bleeding from her powdery knee in runs of black blood. It stung to the touch. And there were people in the parking lot looking, reaching out to touch her and asking if she was okay. They asked if she needed an ambulance.

Eleonore said nothing to them. She only shook her head and pushed them away and walked up to the room and fell into bed as one suffering from a grave illness. It was hard to sleep. And it felt like the bone somewhere in her lower back might be broken.

Soon, Eleonore woke up screaming from a nightmare about Beau being risen from the dead and chasing her across their property. In the dark, the woman groped for her Bird but found only the cold air of the empty place next to her on that mattress and wondered about the money and reached up into the closet where Bird had placed it and found that it was gone. And she was standing in the dark smoking. And she was pacing the parking lot in the morning darkness. And she sat in the room and slumped and was asleep, again, whimpering the way dogs do. The window was open. And a slow drizzle started.

ELEONORE STOOD ALONE IN THE GREY MORNING LIGHT. She was smoking and leaning over the banister. A distant rooster crowed—so faint as if not to be heard at all. And soon, there was movement from one room on the first floor across the courtyard, and a man opened his door and closed it. Then, another tenant with a bald and spotted head ringed in strands of lint-like hair came out of his room to sit in his boxers and smoked and scowled and was scowling so intensely that he looked like he might die of it. He held a magazine in one hand. His fingers twitched. And the sun seemed to be waning before it ever came out that morning, and the world was grey and murky, sunken in an old puddle or pool. Again, the rooster crowed. It was so slight that Eleonore wondered if it actually happened or if it was her mind tricking her or some emaciated memory of the farm she lived on all those years come to haunt her.

Slowly, more and more, the tenants of the hotel reluctantly slid out like disfigured citizens of some deformed dream or survivors of an ancient apocalypse disturbed by their and Eleonore's misplacement in the hotel. They rubbed their eyes.

They spat and limped out of the holes they called rooms and sat and looked up at the sky as if bothered by the sun in its remoteness and stood like loiterers and blinked at the ground or at each other. And there was a neckless middle-aged woman with thin red hair and a hideous archipelago of moles and hair down her neck wearing a muumuu who bore more resemblance to a refrigerator or moving truck than she did any human Eleonore had ever seen. The woman breathed loudly. Her every movement seemed to exhaust her. And soon, on the same woman's step, sat a younger girl—possibly a daughter—who had red hair, also, and what looked to be mosquito bites all over her face and arms and a bald-headed baby bouncing and slobbering in her lap. The young mother of the babe smoked. The pock-faced girl would talk and joke in a heavy southern accent, trying to keep her mouth shut and blushing when she showed her teeth in a moment of laughter or flashed her grim-toothed grin. Sometimes, she was coughing and spat. And the wide, older woman's mouth was open so that she could breathe, and the fat woman was leaning, and she was sweating. She swallowed air with her mouth.

Another spindly limbed man stood on the porch just outside of his room above theirs. And his skin was green or so it seemed. And he was carrying on in conversation with people—whom Eleonore could not see—somewhere above his head and to the left. And next to his room was another door, outside of which sat a dead tree in a pot which was full of plastic trash and bits of foil. Every few minutes a brown, withered face opened the door and peaked out of it as if he were terrified or some kind of overgrown vermin or other self-aware abomination afraid to show himself to the world. And sometime around noon, a man with milk blue eye balls sat blindly smiling and smoking. One man stood, young and healthy, but was strange and feminine. A quiet girl with a flat face sat behind him in a lawn chair and ate dirt and an orange without peeling it and stared up at Eleonore and looked away and stared, again. People came. People went.

Others read from magazines and pointed and talked about things Eleonore could not hear. They were standing. Some were sitting and smoking or not, but all were waiting. Even if they didn't know it, every one of them was miserable and waiting for something like the languishing inhabitants of purgatory itself, and Eleonore was one of them. She was standing on the porch or sitting in the room and smoking, always smoking. And she was waiting, just like they were.

Further on into the afternoon, the door next to hers opened and from it a greasy man—with one scarred eyeball and a nub where his lower leg was supposed to be—hobbled out. He was a veteran of war. The face was red in places and creased with a restless sort of sleep, and he told her that he was a lapsed Catholic who was on his way to hell and was leaning on a wooden crutch.

"For what?" she asked.

"For sleeping. I've gone to sleep and won't wake from it."

"Oh?"

"God doesn't send us to hell so much as he sends the false images we create to hell, the thing we pretend to be or become or fall into being, the artificial creatures and filth in which we shroud ourselves. Like me, God don't want to send little Levi Crum to hell. Levi Crum was a baby, once..."

"Levi Crum?"

"That's me..." The man said drawing his words into a hiss and pressed his dirty thumb into the hair of his chest. Spittle formed at his lip.

"Oh." Eleonore was slapping at a mosquito on her soft white leg and studied the fat dimples behind her knee and was crossing her arms.

"...or who I was, anyway, now I'm just a dope fiend, a derelict cretin down here scouring the world for whatever balloon I can find to pop and sleep, just to wake up and find another to pop it and go back to sleep, again, forever if I could. I love to sleep. And even if I got to him and found him on his dread judgment seat with a sour look on his face about what I've become and all the hop and all the sleep, I still wouldn't turn from it. I wouldn't repent of my sins and I wouldn't give him my needle. No, ma'am. Not at all." His fingers trembled as he dropped the filter of his cigarette from his fingers and reached out and placed his hand on the floor and moved it and did it again and once more until he possessed the cigarette and put it to his lips and smoked.

"How do you know you would not repent?"

"Because I ain't now. This is the time to do it, now's the chance. But put me where I belong. Let Death and Hades swallow me up into their bellies and throw me with them into that lake of fire forever and ever."

Eleonore hummed a beat and was going to speak but had nothing to say and pulled a cigarette from her pack and offered one to the man who took it. And they were smoking in the quiet for some time. But a bird landed on the railing and flapped its wings, and the girl who ate dirt and rinds of oranges was laughing loudly and looking up and pointing at Eleonore who smiled sadly back to the child.

The man on his crutch began to speak, again, calmly, asking,

"And what are you doing, here?"

"Me?"

"Yeah. You. What're you doing?"

Eleonore looked all around. She saw the mindless moving bodies of the other tenants and shook her head and was sad and admitted,

"I'm... um, I'm waiting. I guess."

"What for?"

"I don't know."

"What do you mean you don't know?"

"What about you? What are you doing here?"

"I'm waiting myself, just like you."

"What are you waiting for?"

And for some moments, the man looked at her and smiled and said,

"Supposed to be the Beatific Vision, I think. But I won't never see it. Like I said."

"Be...be... uh, what did you say?"

"The Beatific Vision. What we Catholics, even us lapsed ones, believe the good children of the Lord see when they die and go to..." the man looked up and pointed with his thumb at the sky and clicked with his tongue. "Blessed are the pure in heart: for they shall see God. But I'm not waiting for it, won't never see it..." He paused and stared and went on, "For my man. I'm waiting for my man. Comes by every other day after six. Say, uh, you wouldn't want to buy a typewriter, huh?"

"Typewriter... no. I don't think... I don't think we need one."

"We? I'm asking you."

"Well, no, I mean... I don't see what for."

"It's nice...new, too! An electric Smith Corona," the man held his hands as if he were typing and winked.

"No. Thank you, anyway."

"You look tired," he said. "Or sad or something. Is that you who's always fighting, with the, uh... with the uh the one who sounds different, sometimes like a boy trying to be a man and sometimes like something else? Bird... is it?"

Eleonore shuffled her feet and pressed her hands together and touched her cheek and stared at the pigeons on the roof. She shook her head and swallowed a sob. Now, tears ran. And she was hiding her face and pushing blindly back into her room and was crying and turning on her mattress, waiting for Bird, waiting for someone she wasn't sure would return, someone she wasn't sure had ever existed.

THE DAYS PASSED. They passed just as that first one had without Bird—day after day after day—only slower and more dire for Eleonore who moved quietly around the room and found some remainder of the cash, enough to buy a ride from a neighbor to the store and some food and cigarettes. And one morning, she woke up to a pounding at the door. Two men in coats and short cut hair introduced themselves as officers or agents or something like that. They asked if she had seen or knew of,

"This girl, right here," and they showed a picture of the blonde girl with whom Bird had left.

Eleonore denied that she had with her words and nodded as she said them. They muttered to themselves and spoke with her and asked if they could come into the room. She stuttered and turned away and patted her hipbone. The men left when Eleonore said they could not. And that afternoon, after almost two whole weeks of being gone, Bird straggled back to the room and looked down and had bruises and bite marks on her neck and smears of lipstick on her chin and chest and was without any money. Eleonore hugged her. Both cried, before Eleonore recounted the visit from the lawmen.

Bird stopped twice while they packed and cried to Eleonore, promising to never do it, again, promising to never leave her lover like that. Eleonore said nothing. She was biting the skin on the insides of her lips and cheek and knew that she was, in truth, crippled and dependent on Bird, because she could not live in the world alone as she had while Bird was gone.

She could not make it without her lover, so that no amount of abuse or mistreatment could make her leave. She could never leave Bird. And soon, they were in the Buick and driving on the highways in a cold, mid-September rain in the Pacific northwest.

IN DENVER, Eleonore's shin itched. She scratched the newly forming bump and wondered what it was. And in the northeast corner of New Mexico,

Eleonore thought to ask questions she didn't want the answers to—whether or not Bird loved that other girl or if she had been with others while gone and where the money went. There was nothing to be said. So, instead of asking, Eleonore stewed on her bitterness and waited and laughed when Bird made jokes or hugged her.

In Shreveport, the bump on Eleonore's leg grew and itched more. In Baton Rouge, it was an open lesion leaking a bit of fluid. And the women were in New Orleans by Friday night. There were promises made, again, that all would be better and different, and they both believed it and loved each other. It was calm between them. With some of the remaining money, they rented a small wisteria covered house on Panola Street off Carrollton Avenue where they took long, slow walks at night into a park of Sego palms and Live oaks and Water oaks. In evenings of violet light, they walked hand in hand through the park and sat on the black, wrought iron benches and stared up at the sky or watched traffic and trolleys passing by. And for a moment, the one woman's palm sweating in the other's fingers on the bench, it was as it had been. They had—once more—what was lost when Beau showed up in Idaho and Eleonore fled as a fugitive from her estate. Eleonore rested her ear on Bird's shoulder and breathed.

And on the walk back home—as Eleonore prepared herself to reveal the severity of the unexplained wound on her leg to Bird and suggest that it might be time to see a doctor—Bird spoke, saying she was taking the car,

"To go get another shoe... You know..."

"Oh, yeah... sure. Okay. Here," Eleonore said,

scared to hand over the keys.

"See you in just a bit, baby. Get some rice and a shoe and be right back," Bird said and kissed Eleonore's head.

But instead of coming back right away, as Bird said she would, Eleonore spent nine days alone and suffering and staring at the yellowed wallpaper slowly sloughing off of the walls in the bedroom. It was on the second floor. There were cock roaches everywhere. And the leg had swollen to well over twice its size, so that Eleonore could not walk and was alone, sweating and shrinking dramatically on the bed.

When Bird came back on the tenth day, the thing on Eleonore's leg had opened up into a deep and wet, yellow wound. It was gaping. Translucent chunks of gristle could be seen. There were darker red bits of tissue, muscle and tendon and whatever else. In one place, opaque white bone showed mutely. And as Bird came through the open bedroom door, haggardly offering up words she intended to say but couldn't as she gagged at the smell in the room. It was a grave thing to behold.

THEY SAW A SMALL DOCTOR with small hands and a small face in Kenner, an old river town a block from the levee. He pushed the dull nose of a syringe into the sore where fluid had collected and drew it into the glass cylinder. It was a long process. After an hour of Eleonore screaming weakly and feebly squeezing Bird's hand, they left with a few prescriptions and filled them and returned to the house. They slept. Eleonore could not walk. Her joints swelled. A fever ran its course, and she screamed in her sleep about Beau.

The woman with the grievously cankered leg

ate as food was pressed to her lips and drank. She healed. But she never spoke to Bird. She was weak. And not one more week passed before she woke up to find herself alone, once again abandoned by her miscreant lover. And Bird repeated a saying, over and over, as if she were saying it to Eleonore but seemed to be more a mantra for herself. She said,

"I promise, E. I promise you, if I do it again, you can leave."

But in a few days, hours after Eleonore sat at the flimsy table in the kitchen and ate a sardine sandwich—something substantial for the first time since arriving in New Orleans—Bird was gone, again. This time it was for two nights and most of another day. And on her return home, there was no consolation. No words sufficed to mend the hurt, then. Eleonore limped as she paced and made fists and raised her voice. She stomped her foot and punched a wall.

Blood vessels popped in one's face as she screamed. And there was a slap. And there was a scuffle and hair pulled. And now, they fought hard like men, the shorter, fatter woman charging as bulls do and the taller, uglier woman swinging fists and coffee cups at her head. Fabric ripped. A head and then a foot put holes into the drywall which crumbled into their eyes. Blood ran and soaked into their clothes and was in their mouths, so that they spat sprays of blood into one another's face.

Then, it was screamed that Bird was not a man at all and could never give the other woman a child and what was a lover to a woman who could not sire children. Bird choked Eleonore. Her hands were around her throat for a long time, so long that both thought she would die. Now, they lay collapsed in a heaving pile of flesh on the filthy floor, there. It was done. The fight was over.

They sat up with bloody faces. Bird found a pack of cigarettes and lit two, handing one to Eleonore who shook her head and blew air from her nostrils and shook her head, again, and took one, anyway, and smoked it. None spoke. The sewer smell of Bird's breath hung in the air between them. For an hour, Eleonore dressed and packed. And both had washed themselves.

As the car was running, as the fatigued Eleonore moved things from the house into it, Bird sat watching, defeated and dejected. It was a long time without any talking, or so it seemed to the women. And now, Eleonore stood with her back to the door and faced Bird with her hands on her hips—rubbing the leg which she held up off of the floor—and said,

"Well, are you coming or what?" because she wasn't really going anywhere, anyway, not without her lover.

Bird didn't speak. She smoked and slumped her shoulders and winced with sadness and was crying full tears. And soon, so was Eleonore. The women stood there looking at each other in the front room. Eleonore was studying the masculine gaps in Bird's square teeth and the grease-caked collar on the shirt of her lover. There was a desire to make it all work—to endure with Bird. And though she understood perfectly her inability to live alone, as she had before Bird, Eleonore's passion had gone from her. She felt little. There was no anger or hurt or love or desire to serve her and be the odd trophy she'd made herself for Bird or anything else, anymore—the things which had been everything were gone, and there was nothing, now. She realized that was why she was crying. She was lamenting the loss of her passion.

And looking into Bird's lucid brown eyes and smelling her breath, she understood that she had the upper hand.

Now, Eleonore was on top.

THEY STAYED AT THE HOUSE. And now, there was no worry about when or if Bird would leave. She would not. She could not. And Eleonore knew it.

Bird all but knelt at the foot of the bed, as Eleonore rested—better but still recuperating with her leg. And Bird leaned forward watching her sleep from a chair in the corner and brought her food and water and counted her pills and doled them out to her as the prescriptions on the bottles instructed. Sometimes, Bird combed Eleonore's hair—now half black and half its original bland colorlessness where it had grown out of the scalp. Or she rubbed Eleonore's feet and neck or wiped her face with a wet rag and walked her afflicted lover to the shower and helped her make toilet. Sometimes, she cried. The dark-haired woman wrapped her long fingers around Eleonore's feet and pressed her forehead to them as if in prayer to a savior. She told her she loved her. Bird was always saying it.

But over time, Eleonore's countenance—the disinterest in the face and unreciprocated affections and absence of the words, "I love you," on her lips—wounded Bird. Then, she stooped to a desperate groveling—seized up in grief over it. And other words came out of Bird now. She said,

"I'm sorry," all of the time. It was always, "I love you," or, "I'm sorry." And she might crawl into the bed and fall pathetically on top of a tensing and grunting Eleonore. Or Bird might let out absurd sobs and squeal in the corner or try to press her snotty nose and mouth into Elenore's temple who would shake her head and angrily protest, until Bird was once again standing on the threshold of the bedroom saying,

"I'm sorry. I'm sorry. I'm so sorry, Eleonore."

As if tired of having the mess of hot snot and tears pressed into her cheek and hearing the pathetic words from Bird, Eleonore brought up other subjects. She asked Bird about her life. And she talked about how she was,

"...tired of the hot around here, Bird. We just did summer. Don't you think it's time we had some winter." And the subject of where they might go next came up.

"Where do you want to go, E?" Bird asked.

"Anywhere cooler than here. It's October. Feels like July. Where can we go? Is there anywhere?"

"I don't... I don't know, really..." Bird walked away. With her back to Eleonore, Bird stared into the black hallway and smoked a cigarette and grabbed her wrist behind her back. "Mmm... maybe, I have a place."

"That's where, again?"

"Northwest."

"Northwest?" Eleonore winced, looking at Bird like she couldn't believe what she was hearing. "Are you sure about that?"

"Well..." Bird was grasping for an answer—to prove her worth—and spoke with an air of self-importance that made Eleonore turn her head, unable to bear the sight of it. "...well, I think, if I remember correctly, there was a woman. I knew her son. I think..."

"You think what?"

"I don't know. I think if we go there and say we need help and a job and place to stay, they'll help. How much money do we have left?"

Eleonore grimaced and thought and said,

"However much we need to get there, I'm sure, plus a few months' rent and more."

Bird was licking her lips. Her eyes were red and swollen. She looked desperate—ugly and vulnerable—approaching the bed and hesitating, trying to read Eleonore as she turned off the light and said,

"Okay. How long do you want to stay here? Till we have to go or pay more rent or what do you want to do?"

"Tomorrow's good with me. I'm happy to leave whenever. Put on a coat and stop sweating for a minute. New Orleans has been terrible for me."

There was a long pause. Both women blinked.

"Okay, then. Tomorrow it is." Bird said falling into bed next to and staring at her tired lover.

Eleonore sighed in approval nodding her head and turned her back to Bird and pulled the beaded chain on the lamp and said nothing. She was snoring in a minute.

AND THEY DROVE FOR DAYS AND NIGHTS and most of another day before stopping to rent a stand-alone garage of sorts with a leaky toilet and half ring of a dingy brown gauze in the window screen where a fan had pushed dust through it. The shack sat under tall and heavy trees. It was at the back of an old neighborhood—the kind built decades earlier for the communities formed around the local factories and mills.

Now, the whole lot of houses was sinking. They sank into the black, wet soil beneath the grass. They were small and brittle, twisted homes. Some were abandoned. Some were neglected, and all of it was testimony to the fact that times had changed and were still.

White picket planks were missing from the fence

around the house behind which they lived. An old wooden gazebo lay in ruin, moldy green and rotten and swallowed up by the vegetation. And they paid 45 dollars a week. There was a small stove and sink in the place. Their landlord was a shorthaired elderly woman named Ruby whose two adult daughters lived at home and never came out of their room and were described by their mother with a frown and shake of the head as being touched.

And the fear of the law coming to get them or finding them there—wherever it was, Eleonore did not exactly know, other than a neighborhood referred to as Millwood and that the main and closest thoroughfares were called Argonne and Trent—remained. The Buick was parked down the street, several blocks away. It sat in the street next to a church or behind the school not far away. And Bird disappeared in the mornings. She was working for Mark—Miss Ruby's oldest and only son—doing construction. Her body and bones hurt. The knuckles on her dry hands bled at night, and she was dirty, so that Eleonore felt compelled to wash her and clean her clothes and prepare whatever modest meals could be made from the groceries Bird brought home with her wages.

And on their second Friday in the new place, Bird put on a new button up shirt with a sharp collar. She told Eleonore to get dressed up, to put on wig and fake glasses and look,

"...real feminine for me...like the woman you are..." which Eleonore did and found herself blushing and holding her breath as she bathed and dressed and put her hand in Bird's. And they were walking down the street. It was cold outside. Their breath was visible.

They turned in at a small Italian restaurant with a

black and white tile floor in the waning daylight and cold and ate a rich dinner. Eleonore ate things she'd never had in her life. She squealed with delight. She was laughing and looking at Bird's hands and talking softly. And it was close to ten at night when the owner came out from the kitchen with a towel hanging from his waste and wiped his hands and asked how the two sisters enjoyed their meal. Now, the check came and Bird paid for it with several bills she pulled from her pocket.

Outside in the streetlight, the thin disheveled figure held something out to Eleonore in her hand, presenting her with a memory she had forgotten. It reflected yellow light. It was the ring which had been taken from her finger all those months prior and never given back. Now, Bird said,

"I took this from you. I think I took a lot from you, now, and maybe some of that was ok. Maybe, some of that was what you wanted. Most of it you probably didn't, but here we are. And...um...well, I want to...um..." She was fumbling for words.

Eleonore stared at her. Her mouth was open.

"...give it back to you. You deserve better, E. You always have. And I know we've held so much jewelry in our hands that this thing here..." Bird reached into her breast pocket and pulled from her jacket a box and opened it, revealing a cheaper ring. "...this thing isn't really that much. But I worked for it. And it's honest, and it might be the only honest thing I've ever done in my life, so I want you to have it. I want to give it to you." And with that, Bird was kneeling in a cold puddle on the sidewalk looking up pleadingly and asking, "Eleonore Smith, will you marry me?"

"Marry you?" Eleonore put her hands over her mouth.

"Will you marry me? Let me make you honest. Let me be your man. And you can be my wife."

There was no word from Eleonore.

"Please?" A tear moved in Bird's eye. "Please, E. I love you."

And with that Eleonore put her hand out. The ring slid onto her finger.

FOR THE DAYS THAT FOLLOWED, Eleonore saw Bird—and herself—differently. She saw Bird stripped bare. The slender frame of the woman who Eleonore watched and called her man had found a new existence apart from her flaws and mistakes and crimes, the abuse she had heaped onto Eleonore for so long, now. There was a vision of who she was before the world had disfigured her, the child untouched by the cruelty and world which had deformed her so long ago.

To Eleonore, the breath was neutralized. The thick hair on her body and the plaque on her toenail was, in some strange way, beautiful and manly. And it was, again, a time when Eleonore truly served her mate as she would have desired to serve any man whom she called husband. She knelt and untied Bird's hardly-scuffed work boots. And she remembered how foolishly she'd been taken by the whole experience so early in their acquaintance back at the farm in Idaho. Eleonore seemed another person, then, a child led by the burning of her members and the impassioned rapture of those first months around Bird. It was clear, now, how much of her initial feelings—which later developed into a sick obsession and devotion—for Bird was only her own desire to be desired. That was it. That was what drew her to the stranger in the first place.

And now, she saw herself as older. She was more mature. The suffering they shared—the ways they had violated and hated each other over the last year—and the commitment to reconcile themselves, one to another, bred true intimacy between them. Though the paranoia of the consequences they deserved for their crimes remained, Eleonore found herself at peace and accepted Bird as she was. For both were injured in some way.

Both were marred by the world, and now, when Bird wanted to drink, again, she would confess it, and the women would walk to the store in the sleeting rain and buy a bottle to drink huddled in each other's arms down by the river, close to their little home. Sometimes, when she was drinking with Eleonore, Bird said crazy things.

On a dark Sunday afternoon, she said, in a drizzle,

"Our love has come to an end, E. I think it's over... we can't. You... you can't keep on with me."

"What are you talking about?" Eleonore asked and slapped Bird's chest and shook her head.

"I can't help it. I can't..."

"Can't help what?"

Bird held out a clear pint bottle and twisted the cap off and said,

"I can't... I won't hurt you like I have. Here it is. This is me, and I'm a drunk. This is all I am. Now, drink with me, my woman. Our love is at an end."

And Eleonore drank. She pushed her face into Bird's chest and wiped her cheeks on the soft fabric of the shirt and smelled the stink of her lover's breath and clasped her hands behind Bird's back beneath the heavy coat. And it was drizzling, and Bird's voice strained,

"When you're gone. I'll come down to the water here, this river, and think of you, and one day, I'll walk in it and drown myself, because I won't have you."

The taller woman sobbed quietly. Now, they walked home together. There was a great knocking in the trees of branches against branches, and smaller branches flew through the air, so that the women hunched and shielded their faces. A windstorm was kicking up bits of gritty mud from down the street.

And in their bed, something was clapping violently outside—a neighbor's shutters. Old Miss Ruby's windchimes swung high and crashed in the yard from her porch. And Bird was with Eleonore. She was warm and yawning and drinking and nodding. And Eleonore was with her, smiling and trimming the wet and tattered fray in the heels of her lover's khaki pants with a pair of scissors, and she reached out to Bird and took her hand. And she was warm and soon snoring. The radio played quietly through the racket of the storm outside. Soft orange light emanated from the bathroom. Another type of light came from the tall brass lamp standing in the corner. And the girls were together and soon drooling on their pillows as they slumbered the way old married couples who have fought for their marriage do. They had found love.

SHE WAKES IN THE DARK but for a little light. Cold water has soaked from the other side of the bed onto her clothes, and she pinches the fabric. Something warmer and thick and liquid is on her shoulder. Whatever it is smears in the darkness like blood and smells of iron and is blood. Her fingers touch the cool skin of a chin bone—a rigid lip and teeth—moving freely and hauntingly and turning completely in her hand as something unattached to anything. It falls off of the bed. She reaches for it. There are teeth, again, and flesh. And she reaches over to where Bird's face should be or her pillow or shoulder. It is only the knotted wood of giant tree trunk and cold water running down her arm.

Now, she stands and feels around the room. The air is moving. It is hard to breathe, and when she finds the lamp and pulls the chain and can see, the light shows Bird's arm and top half of her body cartoonishly smashed by and sticking out from under the massive tree and pieces of the roof and ceiling which are all caved in on the other side of the room, and where the woman's body had been when they fell asleep, it is not, now. Other than hairy scalp of the detached skull and blood and an arm, only Bird's lower legs and feet show, clad in tight striped socks—grotesquely twisted and distorted by the violence of the tree's fall. The back wall is missing. White brick rubble strewn across the yard is all that remains. The cold and wet wind takes her breath.

And now, as if momentarily blinded and unaware, she is transported instantaneously and finds herself outside of crushed dwelling and staring back at it. In her hand is that ornamented lock of hair from the mangled body of her now dead lover. The pair of dirty red high tops are on her feet. But she can't remember putting them on her feet or climbing through the window or how she'd found anything. A small bag is in her hand. It has the keys to the Buick and some clothes.

She moves through the neighborhood. And this is the end of all things, or so it seems to be for her. And the early morning light is darkened in the sky. A plague of roofing tacks and heavy roofing shingles descend upon her, pelting her. A roof rolls across a yard and flops into the street on top of a car. She leans into the storm and screams.

In places among the black houses of the neighborhood, sparks flash and pop from downed powerlines arcing on metal fences or against children's swing sets, kicking up the noxious, chemical smoke of burning metal and rubber. And there is the audible and violent buzzing of those fallen cables like wild tentacles of the sky itself thrashing through the yards and streets, as if searching from someone or something to electrocute. She is terrified. She is screaming and hiding her face with her white hands.

Out of the neighborhood and closer to the train tracks where the Buick rocks in the wind, there is light. It is grey. She turns to see three trees lying through a number of houses. Where they've come out of the ground, there are great balls of the soft black soil—thick, gnarled roots with thinner, paler roots that hang from the masses, kinked and stringy like tapeworms in dung. And she takes shelter in the car. It lists in the wind. Those two tons of steel move as if to levitate. There are a pair of trashcans tumbling past her. One smashes the car.

And another giant crash happens somewhere but cannot be seen, only heard. The wind pushes puddles across the asphalt. It pushes them up to the curbs so that they seem to be alive and crawling on their bellies like an intermediate species—legless and giant pseudopodal creatures— desperately fleeing the wrath of the very being which has given them life and now seeks to kill them for their wickedness.

And it is still. It is quiet, for a moment. And now, an angry spit of wind makes a cyclone of rocks along the train tracks and gyrates and twists toward the car. Now, in violent orbit around the twisting thing, something white—perhaps a bag of trash or ragged Styrofoam box—whips around in a large circle across the tracks and back and across the tracks again and crashes through the window of the Buick, so that she can see the thing has feathers and a beak and is bleeding. She sees that it is a duck. And it is dead. And after that, she gasps for air but finds none in the hostile atmosphere.

WHEN IT STOPPED, the sky was crisp and blue. Birds chirped wildly as if communicating unbelief to each other and to the woman as she stood outside of the car and staggered and leaned on the hood and grabbed the dead bird from the back seat and tossed it onto the ground. It was sunny outside. She had been badly scratched by the debris and branches of the tree that had fallen on her lover the night before. Now, trees and powerlines or pieces of fence cut off all passages out of the neighborhood. She travelled a few blocks and was stopped.

Soon, she was stuck, again, at some new dead end where the frazzled inhabitants and grimacing owners of the pulverized and wasted homes—the parents and children who'd slept under the flattened roofs—milled about in the streets wincing or squinting as they leaned in to see or hopelessly held their hands on their hips as they commiserated in whispers over the destruction and what it would mean for them. She stared at them and their loss, stark eyed herself and burdened by the pain of her own.

Though, she was, yet, unable to consider it. Bird's brutal death existed was a thought which she could not ponder—a reality cocooned somewhere in her mind, unseen and untouched, yet hanging silently there for her to open when the time came. Grief would break her when it was.

Finally, after some hours, she made it to Trent Avenue. Travel did not open up. Movement was no freer there than in the neighborhood. There was traffic. Horns beeped. Thick droplets of sweat formed on her lip and between the creases of loose skin by her armpit, and she wiped her face with a rag. There was a flatbed truck which had carried bags of concrete, and it had wrecked terribly in the commotion of the storm and was on its side in the intersection. Grey powder which had caked in the rain covered the pavement creating a surreal scene.

Ambulances flashed their lights. Though, the drivers stood lazily watching the mess being picked up and, now, turned on their sirens and crawled on the sidewalks past her as she waited. Soon, she was moving. Soon, she was on the highways and back to the places she'd been with her deceased lover.

FOR A FEW DAYS, she stood in the rains of Olympia and wandered as lost and smote her chest and was in New Orleans, again, with a fever and cough she'd caught in Olympia. This time, she rented a small room above a tavern where only men drank. The patrons of that bar wore leather or little clothing at all and laid bare their hairy chests as they walked arm and arm or followed each other to meet in the bathroom.

She was the only female patron and drank heavily. And there was from her window, the view of a small, dirty courtyard behind the small, dirty bar where a number of tortured statues—noseless and earless and fingerless as if burnt in some eternal and horrible fire—stood or sat dejectedly staring in various directions without purpose, disgusted by their own presence in that quiet company, all looking as if they'd given up, condemned to bear for eternity those jagged streaks of lime and white specked splats of pigeons' droppings in the dreary New Orleans winter. And she slept on a mat by the door.

Her rest was as a tormented soul bereft of its body, no longer able to hide from itself that which it has worked, good or evil. And her sleep was heavy upon her like a man laid low by deep fever and turning upon his sheets as a door on its hinges. She was scratching herself. Her clothes were wet. And the drafts in the room visited her like ghosts and kept her awake. The woman turned. She was itchy and sweating cold and turning. She was always turning.

She drank and stumbled and knew a man—her first—and knew another after him. And she lay on her back on the floor and gurgled at the ceiling and babbled as if invoking through the chaos and incoherent murmurings some ancient ancestor or the very spirit of her deceased lover and stood in the mirror and worked the lock of hair which she'd stolen from the dead Bird into her own and shaved all the rest of it so that only the one lock hung from her scalp. And she touched her forehead as her lover had on mornings that were good. There was something she had never seen in the mirror, yet something she knew, staring back at her. Months passed and were passing.

And a fellow patron of the bar below her floorboards tattooed her with a sewing needle and a sooty mixture of something oily. The man's face was rat-like. And he bit his lip as he scrawled the crude character of a green inked Virgo symbol into her forehead and tattooed the outline of a mocking bird onto her right hand, so that she bore the image of the woman she'd loved in her head and in her hand and was in some way an analogue of that reality and sought to become her and was stricken with grief over her loss.

She was in Nacogdoches after that. She was in Amarillo. She was in Albuquerque and talked to a man next to a burned-out building who wore a raccoon hat on his head and said he was looking for a ride to,

"Taos... you know where that is?"

"No. I don't. I'm not sure where I am, right now." Her voiced had changed, a false southern singsong had found its way into her speech.

"You're in New Mexico. Rio Rancho. Basically, Albuquerque, que no..."

"Okay," she laughed and rolled her eyes. Her head was wrapped in a fuzzy blue scarf. She looked old and small. "No difference to me..."

"You can take me, then? Or what's going on?" The man showed her a pair of skinny, yellow teeth in the early morning light.

"Get in, boy." She slapped her thigh and yelled and was lunatic.

The man tilted his head and smiled,

"Okay, then."

"Okay, then," she mimicked.

And they rode. The proud Spanish singing of Mexican polka played on the radio. Dust and moisture clouded the windshield and smeared as her windshield wipers labored across the glass. It was late winter, and all was mud but the road upon which they travelled. Somewhere before Santa Fe, the man in the raccoon hat asked,

"Say, uh, what's your name anyway?"

"My name?"

"Yeah. What's your name? You got a name, right?"

"Oh, yes. I have a name. But do you have a name?"

"Derrick."

"Oh, hi. Derrick?"

"Yeah. Derrick. What's your name, lady? C'mon." He squinted one eye as if looking upon someone deranged and unattached from reality.

"Well..." she drew the word and reached for the ID card sticking out of the ashtray in the console. A crushed cigarette butt fell out of it as she pulled the card. It was one of the last ones she used in Atlantic City, and the woman frowned at it. Now, she handed the card to the man and said, "You tell me. What's my name? Huh? I want to know. You tell me, boy!"

"Let's see..." the man held the card up to his face scratching his whiskers and squinting. He studied it and slowly said, "Mary... It says Mary Greenbaum. Is that you?"

"That's me."

"What? What is your name, lady? This is wild." He stood partially in his seat and gripped the dash.

"Mary. You can call me Mary..." but she was slower and softer with her voice, as someone working themselves up or memorizing something, and now, she smiled and said to the man quietly and confidently, "My name is Mary. It's a pleasure to meet you, Derrick."

Birch was referring to an incident that happened a half hour earlier. There was screaming and commotion and guards holding a woman back from charging the stand and pouncing onto the defendant—Samantha McCool. The judge had frantically pounded his gavel. He called a recess.

It all started earlier, when the district attorney asked a feeble framed witness—an adolescent girl with bad teeth,

"So...you say that Vivian Varon is not her real name."

"That's correct. Yes." The young witness said so that barely anyone could hear it.

"Can you say that, again, so everyone can hear you?"

"Yuh-yuh-yes."

The prosecuting attorney turned to the jury for a moment and addressed the whole courtroom—full of the plain-faced and drab dress of farm folk and fishermen from the surrounding area.

Those common, antiquated folks were reading about a scandal involving the famed and late Mr. Bernstein's wife. They read about it every morning at their kitchen tables. There were criminal charges against another mysterious stranger to town—a woman who had been living under false pretenses and had several identities. There were allegations that the old widow had been conned. And the word was that all of it had been born from the middle-aged lady's affair with this other woman. The newspaper said it. And so, having nothing else to do in the coldest and rainiest part of the year, the inhabitants of those surrounding, rural areas came to town. They packed the courthouse. They wanted to see what their newspapers had called a carnival trial.

"Did you hear that, folks? Let it be known, ladies and gentlemen, that Vivian Varon is not her real name, at all!" and now, the District Attorney turned back to the frail witness sitting with terrible posture in the box, "Can you tell us what her name is, the one who everyone called... who says she is Vivian Varon?"

"Her name is Samantha McCool."

"Again, so we can hear you, please," the prosecutor slammed a fist on the wood of the witness stand.

"Her name is Samantha McCool," the girl said louder.

The courtroom gasped.

"Samantha McCool, huh?" the district attorney went on with his examination.

"Yes."

"And do you see her in this courtroom, right now?"

"Yes."

"Can you point to this Samantha McCool who has the alias Vivian Varon?"

"Yes," the girl said and pointed at a young woman with the bleached hair.

"Thank you. Let the minutes reflect that the witness pointed to the defendant," the prosecutor said and held up several enlarged, color photos on cardboard showing a number of bird tattoos along the clavicle and arms and another photo showing that the tattoos belonged to that same girl, the one named Samantha McCool also known as Vivian Varon —the 20-something-year-old who would become Birdy to Eleonore Smith years later. Several other large photos of various ID cards were shown. They all had different ages and different names and came from different cities. The women in the pictures of the ID cards had different colored and styled hair. But the nose was the same in all of them. The eyes were always brown. It was same woman in all of them.

And he went on, declaiming to the crowd and jury about the nature of the defendant's crimes, how she'd lied about her identity to get in with the well-to-do families in the area and how she'd snuck into the 50-something year old Mrs. Bernstein's bed while Mr. Bernstein was dying in the hospital. He gestured wildly and pointed at her.

"She then manipulated the widow, implementing Mrs. Bernstein's full authority over the dealership to get the old manager fired and herself hired on under her fraudulent alias, completely unqualified to run any such business." He turned his attention back to the witness, asking, "What were her intentions with the exotic cars? The Rolls Royces and the Maserati?" NOTE

"To sell them."

"And you knew she knew they didn't belong to her, correct?"

"Yes, sir."

"We have a recorded phone call. Play it now!" he screamed to his assistant. Then, he addressed the timid witness, again, saying in hushed and soothing whisper, "And you can tell me if this is indeed a conversation you had with the defendant."

After some moments of silence, a reel-to-reel player which was propped up on a stool had begun to spin and the audio of a phone call between the young witness and the defendant played. It was a scratchy recording. But the gist of it was clear.

The witness was scared. She was one of the voices on the call, and the defendant was reassuring her that the cars were worth more money than she could make in half of a lifetime. As the young witness expressed more doubt and concern about the crime, the defendant—who had spoken with a southern drawl up to that moment—crooned to the girl in another accent and said clearly,

"Listen Erica," which was the witness's name, "You're my baby girl. You are my heart. Don't worry about the old lady. She's helped me get this far, but I can't leave her yet without blowing my cover. I have to wait till Jimbo comes up for the Rolls Royce, at least. Then, I can leave. There'll be two left. You'll drive one. I'll drive the other, and once they're sold, we'll wake up in Acapulco, baby."

"Really?" the smaller voice asked, desperate.

"Really."

"You don't love her?" the words were small and squeaky.

"How could I love a rich old bag like her when I have the most beautiful thing talking to me on the phone, right now?" There was a pause and an emotional breath, a stifled sob, on the line. And the defendant went on, saying, "She's got the money. I don't care about her. I swear it on all that I am, baby, on everything." And the tape stopped.

Gasps and whispers came from the crowd. Next to the bleached blond defendant sat a fat, slick haired lawyer in a dirty suit who had begun to sweat and squirm and wipe his face with his sleeve.

The prosecutor turned to address the staring crowd. Members of the jury murmuring to each other. There was a commotion. The girl on the witness stand half stood to see it. while the public defender and Birdy turned their heads to see, also.

A short woman with a hooknose was tearing off the ragged raincoat hood which had hidden her face. It was Mrs. Bernstein herself. She lunged forward. And she was pressing through the arms

and bodies of the crowd.
The bailiff restrained her.
Mrs. Bernstein thrashed to
get through, one more
time, and fell to the floor
emitting a high-pitched
and gurgling shriek, she
was screaming,

"Call me an old bag, huh?
I'll kill you. I'll kill you."